RAZORBILL

BLUES FOR ZOEY

ROBERT PAUL WESTON is the author of several internationally award-winning books for children and young adults. His first novel, *Zorgamazoo*, won the Silver Birch Award, the Audie Award, the California Young Reader Medal, and an E.B. White Read Aloud Honor. His second novel was the hard-boiled fairy tale *Dust City*, which was a Canadian Library Association Young Adult Honour Book and was shortlisted for both the Red Maple Award and the Edgar Allan Poe Award for Best Young Adult Mystery.

ALSO BY ROBERT PAUL WESTON

The Creature Department

Prince Puggly of Spud and the Kingdom of Spiff

Dust City

Zorgamazoo

BLUES FOR ZOEY

ROBERT PAUL WESTON

razor bill

RAZORBILL

an imprint of Penguin Canada Books Inc., a Penguin Random House Company

Published by the Penguin Group
Penguin Canada Books Inc.
90 Eglinton Avenue East, Suite 700, Toronto, Ontario, Canada M4P 2Y3

Penguin Group (USA) Inc., 375 Hudson Street, New York, New York 10014, U.S.A.
Penguin Books Ltd, 80 Strand, London WC2R 0RL, England
Penguin Ireland, 25 St Stephen's Green, Dublin 2, Ireland (a division of Penguin Books Ltd)
Penguin Group (Australia), 707 Collins Street, Melbourne, Victoria 3008, Australia
(a division of Pearson Australia Group Pty Ltd)
Penguin Books India Pvt Ltd, 11 Community Centre, Panchsheel Park,
New Delhi – 110 017, India
Penguin Group (NZ), 67 Apollo Drive, Rosedale, Auckland 0632, New Zealand
(a division of Pearson New Zealand Ltd)
Penguin Books (South Africa) (Pty) Ltd, 24 Sturdee Avenue, Rosebank,
Johannesburg 2196, South Africa

Penguin Books Ltd, Registered Offices: 80 Strand, London WC2R 0RL, England

First published 2014

1 2 3 4 5 6 7 8 9 10 (WEB)

Copyright © Robert Paul Weston, 2014

ONTARIO ARTS COUNCIL
CONSEIL DES ARTS DE L'ONTARIO

Manufactured in Canada.

LIBRARY AND ARCHIVES CANADA CATALOGUING IN PUBLICATION

Weston, Robert Paul, author
Blues for Zoey / Robert Paul Weston.

ISBN 978-0-14-318328-0 (pbk.)

I. Title.

PS8645.E87B58 2014   jC813'.6   C2013-906728-0

Visit the Penguin Canada website at **www.penguin.ca**

Special and corporate bulk purchase rates available; please see
www.penguin.ca/corporatesales or call 1-800-810-3104, ext. 2477.

FOR ANYONE WHO PLAYS—ANYTHING

In the brightness of life
In the dimness of dreams
In Heaven, on Earth
It ain't what it seems

—SHAIN COPE
FREUDIAN SLAP, PART 1

1. This Story Is Not a Mystery

This story is not a mystery. It's a puzzle. A bunch of oddly cut slices of cardboard, jumbled together in an unmarked box. How do you solve a puzzle? You dump the pieces on a table, spread them around in a way that makes sense (or seems to), and then, one by one, you start putting it all together. That's when the trouble starts.

There's a lot of pieces and nothing is what it seems, not when you're holding just one. How do you know which way is up? Is that the blue of the *sea* or the blue of the *sky*? To see the connections, you have to put them in order. Piece by piece. Moment by moment. It's true for puzzles and—that summer—it was true for me, too.

If you're still following this lame puzzle metaphor, you may be wondering, What sort of pieces am I talking about? In this particular puzzle-slash-story, they would go something like this:

1. Fathers
2. Illness
3. Lies

4. Love
5. Money*
6. Murder
7. Music
8. Secrets
9. Sex
10. Sleep

That's the top ten in alphabetical order (which is not to say the alphabet is going to help; it's merely convenient). Why the asterisk beside *Money*? Because even though I might be tempted to say number nine is the most important piece of all, it's not. The most important thing in this story is life's *other* major trip-up. Money. That summer, it ruled my life (and ruined it).

Which brings me to the worst problem of all. Unlike a puzzle, life doesn't come in a neat little box. There's no picture you can look at to tell you where you're headed. Sometimes, you don't even know you're doing a puzzle at all. Not until it's too late.

2. The First Time I Saw Her, Part 1

It was the end of July, the deadest of summer, when Mr. Rodolfo saved money by skimping on air-con at the Sit'N'Spin. That would be the laundromat where I worked part-time during the school year and full-time over the summer. If you've never had the pleasure of folding two hundred ratty towels for the semi-homeless men of the Emerson Centre, here's a tip: don't. It sucks.

That day, the only do-it-yourselfer was an old lady at the back. She moved so slow, I worried she was on the verge of a stroke. She kept dabbing her head with a handkerchief, leaning heavily on Ol' Betty, the store's perpetually broken washer. (It was Sit'N'Spin policy to dump the floor swill down Ol' Betty's gaping gullet whenever the floor was mopped.)

It was just after one in the afternoon. I know this because the Brothers had just left with the Premium Service dry cleaning. Premium Service meant your undies were scrubbed with chemicals in a factory space Mr. Rodolfo rented down by the lake. I'm not sure if the Brothers were genuine twins, but in their baggy workman overalls, they were indistinguishable. Every afternoon, they stalked in like a pair of thugs, rarely saying a word to me, and collected the Premium Service. We so seldom interacted, I'd forgotten their actual names. Joe and George, I think, but they could just as well have been JJ and Gonzo.

I was folding towel two-hundred-fifty-three-million-and-six (give or take) when guess who showed up?

Becky.

She was wearing a baby-blue mini-tee and yoga pants, and I'll admit I got a momentary flashback, a semi-dirty one of us making out on her bedroom carpet. I hadn't seen her in over a month, not since school ended. We had been basically avoiding each other since March—the *eleventh* of March, to be precise—which was when she dumped me.

"*Kaz!*"

She flapped her arm like crazy, as if I wouldn't notice her without a ferocious wave. "You know you forgot your jacket? Digby's been sleeping on it for, like, *months!*" (Digby was Becky's big, butter-coloured Labradoodle.)

The jacket was a woollen, navy-blue peacoat, a hand-me-down I'd inherited when Dad died. I had wanted it back, but I was too lazy-slash-chicken to go reclaim it. I wasn't all that fond of Becky's dad. He always seemed creepily proud of me for dating his daughter. I expected that sort of thing from Mr. Rodolfo, but from Becky's own father? Creepy. I had a strong suspicion he would have made fun of me for getting dumped.

"Thanks," I said. "I was wondering where that was."

"Now you know."

Instead of handing me the jacket, she laid it on the counter, possibly to avoid touching me. I saw what Becky said was true. The coat was indeed covered with the leftovers of Digby's dog-balding.

"It must have been under there since, like, um … since …"

"March," I said. "The eleventh."

"Thanks, Kaz. Way to hold a grudge."

"Only a little one."

The return of my coat got me thinking about Digby. Once upon a time, *I* was the one covered with the dog's unwanted hair. Not so much anymore, though.

Obviously.

3. A Side-Note about Becky Leighton

She was the first girl I had sex with.

I was *her* first time, too, incidentally. Call it a mutually beneficial exchange of virginity-loss. Unfortunately, that was all it was. Just the one time. *Once.*

After that, she dumped me and hooked up with my former—and obscenely wealthier —schoolmate Topher Briggs. Knowing Topher (which I do), it's safe to say that by the time summer started, Becky had garnered *a lot* more below-the-belt experience than I had.

Let's say, hypothetically, there was a *Becky versus Kaz leader board*. It would have looked something like this:

Kaz Barrett: *1.*

Becky Leighton: *10,000,002—with Topher Fucking Briggs, who once-upon-a-time had been my friend, back when Dad was alive and you defined friend as somebody who farted into a pillow and smothered you with it at sleepovers; back when we could afford to live in oh-so-rosy Rosemount, instead of oh-so-shitty Evandale.*

If there's one thing I learned from Becky Leighton, it's that what Mr. Dearborn taught us in his doomed-from-the-start health class is true: you *do* always remember your first time.

In my case, I remember not having a clue what I was doing. I remember being so nervous my teeth were *actually chattering*. And I remember the worst part, which was stabbing around in the dark. Literally. Actually jabbing my hips around, hoping Little Mr. Kaz would instinctively know where he was supposed to go.

In my head, it all made sense. Wouldn't a hundred thousand years of evolution make things work all smooth-like? I figured two people could just get naked, press themselves together and things would, you know, *slide into place*.

Yeah, well, not so much.

It was humiliating. Becky suddenly went, "Wait! Stop! Not there! *Here!*" At which point, she reached down and took hold of Little Mr. Kaz so she could demonstrate. This might have been a wise course of action except for the fact that tugging gently-slash-helpfully on my unit was almost exactly like getting a hand job, something which, at that point, I was *way* more familiar with. Which of course meant it was all over before it truly began. If you see what I mean.

But that was okay. I was optimistic. *Don't worry*, I thought, *maybe the first time was a sort-of-halfway-in mega-fail, but me and Becky are pretty solid. There'll be plenty more chances to get it right.*

Wrong.

Becky dropped me the next day, which does very little for a young man's burgeoning self-esteem.

If you ask Calen, he'll tell you Becky was just using me. He thought all she wanted was to figure out how the plumbing worked. Anybody would do, he told me. And I said, if that's true, then how come she didn't pick someone who *actually knew what he was doing*?!

"You're lucky," Calen informed me. "At least you went and did it already. Alana's making me wait until we go away to university. That's, like, a year and a half from now!"

So why am I going on about Becky so much?

I don't know, to be honest. I guess maybe I want to lay down a little background and besides, she was there when it happened: when I first saw the Girl with the Dreads.

4. The First Time I Saw Her, Part 2

"I found this in one of the pockets."

Out of her purse, Becky took a photograph. It was of me and Dad. We were standing on the courts at DeWinter Hills, the park in Rosemount where we used to play. He had a basketball under one arm and there was a nasty sweat stain spreading down the front of his shirt. His other arm slung down over my shoulders. In the picture, I was six or seven, back when Dad could still outmanoeuvre me, back when it was just the three of us, Dad, Mom and me. Nomi wouldn't have been born yet.

I slipped the photograph back where I knew Becky had found it, in the jacket's inside pocket. Meanwhile, Becky gazed up at the ceiling.

"How's your mom?" she asked.

"Pretty good," I lied.

"So ..." Her eyes wafted down to me in little increments. "You still saving up?"

"I'll have enough by the end of summer."

"Cool. I'm glad."

Was she really? When Becky dumped me, chief among her reasons was the fact that I was too cheap, too obsessed with saving cash. She whined that we never *did* anything, partly because I wasn't prepared to shell out and partly because I worked every day at the Sit'N'Spin. She had a point. Anyway, my cash was destined for a higher purpose.

Becky glanced up at the ceiling again. "Have you told her yet?"

"Nope."

"But she'll take the treatment, right? Like if you have the money?"

"Maybe. She still thinks I'm saving for university. As if they'd let me in anywhere."

From downstairs, I heard the jingle of Mr. Rodolfo's keys. As operator and sole proprietor of the Sit'N'Spin Laundromat, he kept an office down there. I was never allowed inside.

After we closed on Saturday nights, it was down in the basement where he hosted poker games with a bunch of Evandale regulars.

Mr. Rodolfo is a big guy. As he came up the steps, every one of them creaked. He wasn't exactly fat, just thick—thick arms, thick legs, thick neck. He looked like those old wrestlers you see in pictures from the fifties, chubby but solid guys, big kettledrums with arms and legs.

"*Becky!*" he shouted, flashing me a dirty grin. "If only I were young again."

"If only," I said.

"Becky, Becky, Becky!" Mr. Rodolfo slapped the glass of the dry-cleaning booth as he repeated her name. "We haven't seen you in *aaaaages*. You're making your boyfriend here lonely!"

Boyfriend. I winced. (I hadn't gotten around to telling Mr. Rodolfo Becky had dumped me. I had the impression that, a bit like Becky's father, he might be disappointed.) Becky, meanwhile, wasn't impressed. Her eyes tossed a drawerful of knives at me and then whipped a few at Mr. Rodolfo.

"Excuse me?" she asked.

"Don't worry." Mr. Rodolfo started straightening the little one-dollar boxes of detergent on the shelf behind the counter. "This way, your beau here can concentrate on his job, instead of—well, you know, getting all *distracted* with you around."

The knives were growing in size and sharpness. They were now more like a set of katana. "Um, *Kaz?* I think maybe you have something to explain to—"

But she never finished. She never got her chance to spill the beans, because that was when the Girl with the Dreads walked past the window.

5. The Precise Words That Went through My Head When She Walked Past

Holy shit, it's Jesus of Evandale.

6. What My Boss Would Think If Jesus Was a Skinny, Goth-slash-Rastafarian White Girl Who Came with the Craziest Cross in the World

You can't blame me for thinking what I thought. If you'd seen her that morning, you would have thought the same thing.

Because of the cross.

Don't get me wrong. It wasn't like a *regular* cross. Not like a church cross. This was something welded together from the guts of a giant robot, and the welder was obviously a lunatic, probably living in a shack on the edge of a burning forest. It was that sort of cross.

There was sheet metal, driftwood, plumbing pipes, rusty cutlery, crappy toys and bamboo shafts, all hitched together into something that resembled a gigantic crucifix. More junk dangled from the crossbar: chains, cogs, copper wire, knife blades, forks with their tines curled into hooks. There were *bones*, too. All pocked and yellow, like rotten teeth.

The girl's face was in shadow. All I saw were flashes of pale skin under a thick curtain of dreadlocks. They were mostly bleach-blonde, but with a few strands dyed the colours of grape juice and bubble gum. Her jean shorts hung low on her hips, exposing a thin strip of skin between a rainbow belt and the bottom of a black T-shirt that fell off one shoulder, exposing the strap of a pink leopard-print bra (though I'm fairly certain there's no such thing as a pink leopard).

If right at that moment you had told me this person—this goth-rock Jesus freak, half Bob Marley, half Kewpie doll—would spin my life upside down in a matter of weeks, I would have laughed. At the time, however, nobody let out so much as a giggle. Becky was so disgusted by the girl's appearance she forgot all about telling Mr. Rodolfo she had dumped me.

"What a *freak*," she said.

My boss agreed. "She tries coming in here with that thing," he said to me, "you don't let her. Understand?"

I nodded in silence.

"Bad for business." He turned back to the boxes of Tide, sprucing them into rows for the gazillionth time. "Soon as someone like that walks in, you're losing money."

Maybe so, but for some reason, I was curious. Maybe it was her legs, straining under the weight of the cross. In my head, I still saw the streaks of lean muscle flashing up and down her thighs with each step. I went to the window, trying to get a look at her again, but she was gone.

"Get back here," Mr. Rodolfo said. "You're not finished folding. Leaving a pile like this out on the counter—*no way*. Bad for business."

Before I went back to folding, we all heard the pitter-pounding of tiny feet. They were coming down the back stairs. They were *never* supposed to come down the back stairs.

It was Nomi.

7. B-L-O-O-D

My sister burst in through the back door.

"Use the front!" I shouted at her. "You *know* that!"

It was a rule in our house, mostly directed at Nomi: *whenever you go down to Kaz's work, don't go down the back way.* The problem was the rear stairs off our kitchen spat you straight into the alley behind the laundromat. Drivers were always speeding through there to avoid the lights at Steinway and Emerson. (And yes, it meant the three of us—Mom, Nomi and me—lived directly above my work.)

"I'm sorry," Nomi whimpered, "but ..."

"Forget about that," I said, sensing something was wrong. "What happened?"

"It's Mom."

Out of the corner of my eye, I caught sight of Becky, covering her mouth. Only three people outside our family knew about Mom's illness: Calen, Mr. Rodolfo and Becky.

Calen knew because I had known him forever; Mr. Rodolfo knew because we needed to borrow his car whenever Mom went up to Olsten for her therapy; Becky knew because I was dumb enough to tell her when she agreed to have sex with me.

(Afterwards, I made her promise she'd never tell anyone or else I'd start a rumour that she gave me chlamydia. She pointed out that, if I did, then everyone would think I had chlamydia, too. I told her, yeah, that's how badly I wanted her to keep it to herself.)

I didn't tell people because that's what Mom wanted. She was extremely self-conscious about her illness. She doesn't like anyone knowing about it. Probably because of how weird and rare it is.

"Tell me what happened," I said to Nomi.

"Mom told me she was having a nap! She said that's all it was! Just a nap! But then, I couldn't wake her up, so … so I …"

"Take a deep breath."

My sister tried. She opened her mouth but as soon as she inhaled, she started crying. "I tried to pull her out of bed! I just wanted to wake her up, that's all! But she was right on the edge and then I pulled too hard and she hit her head and there's … there's … Kaz, I'm sorry! *There's blood!*"

I had to steady myself. I have this problem with blood. *Hemophobia*, they call it. It means the runny red stuff that keeps us alive is basically my kryptonite. When I see blood, I pass out. The sudden image in my head—Mom's pale face and a red stain soaking into the carpet—made the world turn grey. I shut my eyes tight. I flexed my stomach muscles. I clenched my jaw. (Sometimes that helps.)

When I opened my eyes, Mr. Rodolfo had his phone out, looking annoyed—probably with my lack of action.

"I'll call the ambulance," he said.

8. The Swelling of Sleep

You've heard of appendicitis, right? That *itis* part means to get larger, to swell. My mother has something else entirely. *Somnitis*. It's a rare neurological disease named after Somnus, the Roman god of sleep.

If appendicitis means the swelling of the appendix, I'm sure you can see what somnitis is. It means sometimes my mom doesn't wake up. For days. She can have an attack anytime. One moment she's wide awake, and the next—*zzzzzzzzz* ...

For days.

It's so rare, most people have never heard of it. Not even doctors. Which is why there aren't many working on a cure. There are quacks out there who'd like to sell you crystals or incense or some treatment that includes stabbing you with needles, but none of it works. In those cases, the only people getting well are the "practitioners."

I've read everything about her illness (and I do mean *everything*; there isn't much out there). I've learned that throughout her life, Mom's attacks will get longer and longer. One day, maybe when she's old or maybe tomorrow, she'll fall asleep and never wake up.

9. On Googling

When your mom has somnitis, you can't help but google. A lot.

(Is it just me, or does the word *google*, when used as a verb, sound like slang for masturbation? Example: I'll bet Topher Briggs googles himself, like, ten times a day. See what I mean? This is not to say that there's anything wrong with googling yourself. To quote Mr. Dearborn, my extremely fired health class teacher: "Boys, it's perfectly natural. Everybody does it.")

So like I said, I google a lot. (Please note that I'm now using *google* in the *classical* sense—i.e., searching the internet.) You can't help but type things like, "What is the cure for somnitis?"

The first thing you get is pages and pages of bullshit sites trying to convince you to do more yoga, or get hypnotized, or rub eucalyptus cream on your earlobes. Mom tried all of these, by the way. None of it worked. All it did was teach me my mom's a sucker for miracle cures. It's hard to blame her. She's the one who's sick. When something terrible is happening to you, I guess you're willing to try anything.

Which is why I think it's so crazy she won't try the Sleep Clinic at the Mars-Bowen Health Sciences Complex in New

York City. It's the only Google hit that actually seemed legit. One of the founders is a neurologist who specializes in sleep disorders. These are *actual* doctors. They do *actual* research. Using *actual* science.

On their site, they have a list of everything they have treated, from snoring to insomnia. And guess what? Scroll all the way down to the very bottom and you'll find eight beautiful little letters you won't find anywhere else: s-o-m-n-i-t-i-s.

But there's a catch. Mars-Bowen is one of those all-inclusive, private health complexes. You can only book yourself into the place if you're a member, and membership will cost you. $12,000. Up front.

So now you know what I was saving up for.

10. Big Daddy

In the back of the ambulance, the paramedics had Mom strapped to a gurney. There was a bandage on her head and orange padding stuffed around her face. It pinched her cheeks and pushed her lips into a pair of prunes. But it couldn't stop her from grinning. That was because she was dreaming of Dad.

"Daniel ..." she murmured, breathing deeply. "Daniel ... Daniel ..." She whispered his name over and over. Eventually, the words faded away, but the smile stayed.

The paramedic looked from Nomi to me, arching his eyebrows. "She often talk in her sleep?"

"Sometimes."

I picked up Mom's hand and stroked it. The paleness of her skin looked even whiter under my brown fingers. She squeezed my hand and the grin on her face went even goofier. I think she thought my hand was actually Dad's.

Nomi watched Mom's face, wincing as if in pain. "I shouldn't have pulled her."

"She'll be fine," I told her. "It's not your fault."

Of course, my sister didn't believe me.

At the hospital, they made us sit in an empty hallway while

the doctor did his examination. The blue chairs were a gazillion percent plastic and about as comfortable as the crappy bleachers they have around the track at school.

Nomi sat beside me and kicked her legs, staring at one foot and then the other, swinging up, then thumping against the chair legs.

My sister is eight years younger than me. I was thirteen when Dad died, but Nomi was only five. She says she remembers him, but she doesn't really. (I can match all of her memories to photographs we have around the house, all the ones with Dad in them.)

I worry about her. When you grow up with no father and a mom who's liable to conk out for days at a time, it takes a toll on a kid. Sometimes, I think Nomi's forehead ought to be stamped with the word *FRAGILE*. Everything about her—her arms, her legs, even her hair—seems too thin. The most fragile part of her, though, is her eyes. They're so big and glossy, it's like she's always on the verge of tears.

I put one arm around her shoulders and felt the *thump-thump-thump* as her feet hit the chair. "Don't worry," I said. "Just a matter of time before she wakes up again."

Nomi kept on thumping. "It's because of me."

"You just wanted to wake her up."

"But there was B-L-O-O-D."

"You don't have to spell it."

"But I don't want it to happen to you, too."

I hugged her close. "I'm not gonna pass out just from hearing the word. I promise."

"What if it's not an attack? What if it's because she hit her head?"

"It's just an attack," I told her.

There were televisions bolted into the corners of the room. I thought maybe I could distract Nomi from blaming herself with a TV show. Unfortunately, both sets were tuned into the latest episode of *Big Daddy*, the worst reality TV show ever conceived. They take a bunch of twenty-somethings who have never known their parents, and make them humiliate themselves in competitions to find their biological father.

In the first episode, all of them were exiled on a tropical island (like we'd never seen that one before). They were separated into two groups: orphans who had been abandoned as children and fathers who hadn't known they'd had a kid. The trick is that none of them knew which father had fathered which orphan.

At the end of each episode, all the fathers voted on which orphan they thought was their kid. The orphan with the fewest votes was booted off the show. At the end of each season, the last remaining orphan won $250,000. This was followed by the big revelation scene of which father had fathered the winner. That lucky dad also won $250,000.

I *hated* that show.

"That girl has big boobs," Nomi commented, stating the obvious. On the screen, an orphan in a tank top swung upside down from a tree branch.

"Let's read a magazine," I suggested. I started searching the tables for some kid-friendly reading material, but there wasn't much. Luckily, the doctor came out of the emergency ward. He had a face like a bloodhound, saggy and dull, but reliable.

"You'll be happy to hear your mother's head injury isn't serious. Nothing that would keep her unconscious."

"You see?" I told to Nomi. "It's *not* because of you."

The doctor started asking questions about Mom. *How long*

had she suffered from somnitis? What precisely were the symptoms? Were there any warning signs prior to an attack? At first, I thought he needed this information to treat her properly, but then I realized he was just excited to be treating someone with such a rare condition. To him, Mom was a novelty.

Nomi must have sensed the same thing because she suddenly asked, "Can we go in and see her now?"

11. Some Family History

My mother's name is Aiko, which means "love child." (In Japanese, it isn't quite so hippy sounding. It's just a normal name, like Jane or Sarah. Even still, my mom definitely has some hippy tendencies, and it's possible that was where they came from.) Her great-grandparents came over from Kyoto in the sixties, which makes her a *yonsei*, a term that means "fourth generation." Nowadays, in my family, *yonsei* might be the only word of Japanese any of us know.

The generations that came before my mom were pretty strict about keeping the Japanese bloodline as pure as possible. From the way she explains it, everyone before Mom was under tons of pressure to find a nice Japanese person over here, marry as quick as possible and start popping out little purebred Japanese babies.

That ended with Mom because her parents—my grandparents—both died in a car crash while Mom was studying music at university. As a result, she never had the chance to cave in to parental pressure and hook up with a Japanese guy. Instead, she married my dad. A black guy from

Barbados, which is how Nomi and I ended up several shades darker than Mom.

When I was young, the neighbourhood where we lived in Rosemount was mostly white, so being the colour of a strong latte made you special. Up there, I stood out. In Evandale, on the other hand, just about everybody is some shade of specialty coffee.

When I meet new people, especially adults, I can almost see the wheels turning as they pore over my face, trying to make sense of my puffy lips, my slanted eyes, the freckled blotches that pepper my nose and the tops of my cheeks. Eventually, when they can't figure it out, they always ask the same thing.

"Sorry, I'm just curious, but … where are you from?"

Ambiguous ethnicity also means you get mistaken for everything you're not. People come up to me in the street, speaking some language I can't understand. Sometimes, it's Spanish, sometimes Persian, sometimes something from Southeast Asia. Every time, I apologize politely and explain I have *absolutely no idea* what they just asked me.

Here's something that will never happen:

Stranger on the Street: Excuse me, but I was just wondering, would you happen to be some sort of Japanese-Caribbean half-breed mongrel-type-person?

Me: Good guess.

Stranger on the Street: Huzzah! I knew it! (High-fives nearby friend.)

Yep, never gonna happen.

12. One Way to Become Famous

Nomi and I stood by Mom's bed. Asleep, she looked different. She had been heavier before Dad died. You saw it in photographs we had around the apartment. Mom had always been small, almost as frail as Nomi, but in those old pictures, she at least had a bit of healthy roundness to her cheeks.

That was gone now. The oval of her face had sunk into something closer to a figure eight, her cheekbones caved in and hollow. The bones of her arms—her elbows, her wrists, her knuckles—they all protruded in a way they never had when I was Nomi's age. Now, as I looked at her, lying on a shallow mattress in a cold metallic bed, the only puffiness was around her eyes, swollen with sleep.

Nomi went up and stood beside the bed, but she was still looking at me. "Can I tell her I'm sorry?"

"It's *not* your fault," I told her.

She wouldn't listen. "I'm sorry," she whispered to Mom.

Mom just lay there.

"She can hear us," Nomi said.

"Maybe. Sometimes."

She leaned close to Mom's face. "It's okay to wake up now."

"If only that worked."

Nomi looked at me like I was evil. I was saved from her glare by the buzz of my phone. It was Calen.

"Just calling to check," he said. "You're coming tomorrow, right?"

I was so wrapped up in Mom's attack, I didn't know what "tomorrow" meant.

"It's Topher's party! I'm gonna drive, but I might have a bunch of the team's shit in my car, so I'm trying to figure out how many people I can take. Probably just you. You're coming, right?"

I looked at Mom. If she was still asleep tomorrow, it would be difficult to leave Nomi home alone.

"I might not be able to."

"Dude, no way!" Unlike me, Calen wasn't good on his own. In everything he did, he always needed at least one accomplice. "This is *Toph's* we're talking about."

Every year since high school had started, Topher Briggs had thrown the biggest party of the summer.

"I can't," I said. "I'm at the hospital right now."

"Oh. Your mom?"

"She had an attack today. If it's like last time, she'll be out until Saturday morning."

"Dude. Shit." Calen had a knack for loading a lot of meaning into those two words.

Calen and I had been friends since we were kids, since the time when we were neighbours up in Rosemount. When Dad died, and we moved to Evandale, Calen was the only one who remembered I existed. It's funny how fast people forget you when you're not right in front of them.

"Anyway," I said, "I can't leave my sister alone."

"What if you bring her?"

"Are you insane? I can't show up at Toph's with an eight year old."

"Yeah, I guess."

"*And*," I pointed out, "isn't this whole conversation about how you won't have enough room in your car for anybody else? 'Specially if you gotta drive Alana, too."

"Yeah, but dude, your sister is, like, *tiny*."

"Which is exactly why she's not coming."

"Babysitter?"

"I'll have to let you know tomorrow, but I kind of doubt it'll happen."

Calen said nothing for a second, which at first I took to be silent acceptance, but in fact it was merely a dramatic pause prior to hitting me with a secret weapon.

"You do know that Christina Muñoz is gonna be there, right?"

Christina Muñoz. I had been quietly crushing on that girl—or at least the back of her head—since she sat in front of me in the seventh grade. But ever since we moved to Evandale, I only saw her periodically. At Topher's parties, for instance.

Sadly for me, she was the sort of bright-faced, olive-skinned beauty who emerges from the womb with a boyfriend grafted to the other end of her umbilical cord. Even when we were twelve, she went out with Trevor Greaves for the whole year. Of course, all they ever did was hold hands on the way home from school, but I would've happily taken that much.

"So what?" I said, trying to sound like I didn't care either way. "I think we both know she's gonna be there with some guy."

"Raheem from Central Prep, you mean?"

I had never met Raheem, but I recognized his name. Dating Christina Muñoz made you famous.

"Yeah, him."

"Then this is your lucky day. I heard they broke up, like, *this week*. Which means you have about a three-day window— which means *you have to come*."

All this time, Nomi had been listening anxiously to my half of the conversation. I pulled the phone away and held it against my chest, looking down at her.

"Any chance you could sleep over at a friend's house tomorrow night?"

13. The Second Time I Saw Her

Once Mom was all tucked in at the hospital, Nomi and I left her. She hated it when we waited around, pining for her eyes to open. If she caught us there when she woke up, she'd only be angry.

A streetcar came along just as we got to the stop, and we jumped on. We were coming up Steinway when I spotted her again: the Girl with the Dreads. She was standing out in front of Dave Mizra's jewellery shop. He had closed for the night and, even though it was early evening, the whole block was deserted. All except for her.

Our stop was still two blocks away, so I only saw her as we rolled past. I knew it was the same girl. The same jean shorts, the same eruption of dreadlocks, the same T-shirt dripping down one arm.

She still had the cross, too, only now it was propped up in front of her (in front of her face, actually, so I still couldn't make out her features). She had the butt end of the horizontal bar level with her mouth, almost like she was kissing the end.

It was a humid night, so a bunch of the streetcar windows were tipped open. That was how I realized it wasn't a kiss. She wasn't frenching the cross, she was *playing* it. It was some sort of musical instrument.

Just as the streetcar rounded the curve at Emerson, I saw the horn, something like a bugle or a trumpet, nailed to the crossbar.

The melody she played was a sad one, all in a minor key, slow and kind of beautiful. We only heard a snatch of her music and then she was gone, the streetcar grinding around the shallow corner.

We got off at our stop and I tried to hurry back. I was so curious. Nomi, however, wasn't in the mood to rush.

"*I'm tired,*" she whined.

"It's just two blocks. C'mon!"

Instead, she stopped dead. "Can you carry me?"

Stupidly, I figured with Nomi on my back, we would both go as fast as I could run. When she climbed up, however, I realized I hadn't carried her in a long time. She had grown a lot since then, and it didn't help that she started up with a familiar complaint.

"We used to have a piano, didn't we?" she asked suddenly, speaking directly into my ear. (I wondered if this was the real reason she wanted a piggyback: to get my undivided attention.) "Mom gave you piano lessons, didn't she? When you were my age?"

It was true. Once upon a time, Mom had been a real professional. She gave recitals and had a great job playing with the city orchestra. Back when I was a kid, I worked pretty hard under Mom's tutelage, but I was never any good. I took after Dad more. He was the athletic one. Mom kept trying, though. She never really gave up on me, at least until the somnitis started. Then it all fell apart.

Her first attack was right in the middle of an afternoon performance at Rosemount Concert Hall. Every time I hear that music, my stomach clenches. *Gymnopédie Number 1* by Erik Satie. It was one of her favourite pieces. Halfway through the song, she slumped forward on the piano and … zzzzzzzz.

Nobody could wake her up. She slept for eighteen hours, and the first thing she did when she was conscious again was quit the orchestra. Since then, she hasn't played a single note.

When I was a kid, she always talked about how deeply music affects the human brain. That's why she stopped. She thought the illness was triggered by the music. She believed that by playing just the right notes, in just the right sequence, she had flipped some forbidden switch inside her mind.

Now, she works part-time at the Evandale Public Library. When she applied, she didn't tell anyone there about her illness. Her idea is that if her work environment is quiet enough, *unmusical* enough, it'll prevent anything from happening. So far, it seems to have worked. She still has attacks—obviously—but she's never had one while sitting behind the checkout desk. Between the money from Dad's life insurance and what she earns from the library, we get by.

"Okay, yes," I said to Nomi, "but that was back when we had room for a piano."

"We still have the synthesizer. In the laundry room."

This was also true. In the closet where we kept the washer and dryer, wedged in between the machines and the wall, there was a thoroughly outdated Casio electric piano.

"I don't even know if it still works," I said.

"But you could teach me to play on it. I asked Mom again this week, but she said she can't remember how to do it. She says something's wrong in her head."

"Maybe."

When I came around the bend, I expected to hear the girl's music, but I didn't. The sidewalk in front of Dave Mizra's place was empty. The girl, whoever she was, had vanished.

14. Fire & Ice

The next morning, Mom was still in the hospital. I had the early shift at work, so Nomi came down to the laundromat with me. She brought pillows and a blanket and curled up on one of the benches near the counter. By the time I'd put out the pressed clothes for morning pickup, she was snoozing soundly. About a minute after I had flipped the OPEN sign, Dave Mizra came jogging across the street. Dave lived directly above his jewellery store, Mizra's Fire & Ice. Like half the other businesses on the block, the name was a pun.

Fire = gold.

Ice = diamonds.

Ha ha.

Yes, it's lame, but it's hard to talk when you work at a laundromat called the Sit'N'Spin.

"Kaz-o-matic 3000! Good morning, good morning!" he shouted at me.

I put my finger to my lips and pointed to Nomi.

"Ah, sorry."

Kaz-o-matic 3000 was the nickname Dave Mizra had given me. It was a mash-up of the name on my driver's licence (*Kazuo*, which in Japanese means "harmonious man" and which I almost never reveal to anyone) and the fact that every washer at the Sit'N'Spin was stencilled with the name *Lav-o-Matic 3000*.

He had given himself a nickname, too. His real name was Dodi, but he went by Dave because, as he explained once, in English Dodi sounds too much like a child's toy. Like Lego.

"I am afraid I have only shirts for you today," he said, laying a pile on the counter.

"Premium Service for Delicates?" I asked.

"Of course! *Always* Premium."

"Just these?" I asked.

"Yes," he said, suddenly more solemn than usual. "This is all."

I was surprised. Dave Mizra was known around Evandale for having extravagant taste. He drove a fancy car (an old Mercedes); he wore swanky clothes; he spent tons of money on hair pomade.

It was his clothes, however, that stood out the most. Dave Mizra strutted around the neighbourhood in suits that ranged from shark-blue gangster pinstripes to colourful patchworks of hippie suede, complete with tassels swishing from the arms. This was the reason I knew him so well: his entire wardrobe was dry clean only. So it struck me as odd to see him come in with so small a bundle of clothes.

"Is everything okay?"

He glanced out into the street. "Oh, yes-yes. Everything is perfect."

Dave Mizra is the only person who thinks Evandale is a paradise. He never told me why he left Algeria, but my impression is that it had something to do with a civil war they had in that country back in the nineties.

"I left and because I speak French," he once told me, "I moved to Paris. Over there, the immigration people said I must become a welder. Either that, or drive a taxi. *A welder!* Yes, I work with metal, but I am an artist! So I come here, instead. And I followed my dreams." Whenever he mentioned his dreams, he always pointed across the street.

It was debatable whether or not Dave Mizra was an artist. He designed a few pieces of his own jewellery, sure, but he also had a massive placard out in front of Fire & Ice that read: *WE BUY YOUR GOLD!!!* It wasn't the sort of thing that made you think of Picasso.

The only thing missing from Dave Mizra's paradise was his wife, who was still back in Algeria. A few years ago, they had met here and gotten married, but even though they were hitched, there was some problem with the immigration papers and on their way back from a visit home she was stopped at the border. That was almost two years ago. Dave Mizra had been trying to bring her back ever since.

Of all the things that were interesting and eccentric about Dave Mizra, the oddest thing about him wasn't his clothes, his car, his pretensions of being an artist or his mad idea that Evandale was a paradise. No, the most surprising thing about Dave Mizra was his deep, abiding, seemingly bottomless love of seventies punk rock and glam. Seriously.

Everything I knew about the Ramones, the Clash, David Bowie, Slade, Iggy Pop, Patti Smith, T. Rex, the Jim Carroll Band and so many others, I had learned, improbably, from Dave Mizra. In order to educate me musically, he was always bringing over CDs from his cherished personal collection.

"I have brought you something special today," he said, obviously trying to shift the topic from whatever had him distracted outside. He slid a CD jewel case out of his man-purse and clapped it between his hands, holding it like he was praying. "I think you are finally ready for this."

"Who is it this time?" I reached out for his hands, but he pulled away.

"How do I know you are ready?"

"It would help if I knew what I was supposed to be ready for."

He nodded as if my wisdom had impressed him. "Of course. There is no way to prepare."

He opened his hands and revealed a CD. The plastic case was scratched and worn, but the cover was clear enough. It was a white square printed with something like a Rorschach test, one of those random ink blots a psychiatrist uses to reveal whether you want to have sex with your auntie or just torture rodents.

The blot itself resembled a spider, except each of the eight legs weren't hairy or insect-like. Instead, each one was the bare leg of a woman, complete with eight pointy stilettos. Sprouting from the legs was not one, but two naked torsos. What you ended up with was the silhouette of a twin-stripper-slash-eight-legged beast. In heels.

The only words were at the top, printed in a tiny font like something clanked out of a broken typewriter:

Shain Cope

Freudian Slap

"Kaz-o-matic 3000, it is my pleasure to introduce you to the genius of Mr. Shain Cope."

"*Who?*"

Unlike the other CDs that had come to me via Dave Mizra—all of which had rung vague bells somewhere in the back of my head—I was certain I had never heard of Shain Cope before.

"'*Who,*' he says!" Dave Mizra was clearly disgusted. "In every age, there is a—what do you call it? A maverick. But in those days—*oh*! Everyone was a maverick! That's what made Shain Cope special. Here you have the maverick of the mavericks." He leaned over his pile of shirts and pressed the CD into my hand with both of his. (Dave Mizra is the sort of guy who'll *never, never, never* discover downloads. He's too much of an old-school fetishist for the tattered little booklets that come with CDs.)

I did what I always do when he brings me new music. I turned it over and read the names of the songs, not that the name tells you much.

"'Colt's-Tooth Blues,'" I said. It was the first song on the album. I liked how the consonants bumped rhythmically over my lips. The words kind of forced you to hold the vowels a bit longer, almost as if you were singing. So maybe I was wrong. Maybe you *could* tell something about a song just from its name.

"*Yes*! A classic!" Dave Mizra hummed a bar from a tune I almost recognized. "Do you know this? You must have heard it!" It was the same incredulous question he asked every time he came over with a CD.

I flipped it over again, eyeing the lurid ink blot. Just as I did, Mr. Rodolfo pounded up from the basement. I hadn't even known he was down there.

"What the hell is that?" he asked, looking over my shoulder at the CD case. Before I could answer, he reached over and plucked it out of my hands. After looking at it for a second, he frowned at Dave Mizra. "What're you putting in this kid's head?"

"An education."

"More like insect porn."

Dave Mizra rolled his eyes. "Philistine."

"Wrong," said Mr. Rodolfo. "I'm Portuguese."

Dave Mizra scoffed again and Mr. Rodolfo stalked off to check on the machines. (Whenever he was in a bad mood, he either tidied up or tinkered with Ol' Betty.)

In general, Mr. Rodolfo and Dave Mizra had never really gotten along, but a few weeks earlier, things had hit a new low. The *Evandale Chronicler* published a story about how the lead singer from Wild Blue Bounce had stopped in at Dave Mizra's shop. I wasn't really into the band, but I definitely understood it was a big deal for Veronica Heller to sample your wares.

Dave Mizra had the article posted in the front window of Fire & Ice, which of course made Mr. Rodolfo dead jealous. As I'm sure my boss would say, having a minor celebrity visit your store was nothing if not *good* for business.

"Just listen to it," Dave Mizra told me. "This is music like nothing else."

When he said that—*music like nothing else*—I thought of the girl I had seen.

"Can I ask you something? Have you seen a girl with, like, weird dreadlocks? Hanging around your corner?"

"Of course," he said. "She's my angel."

"Your angel?"

"My *maverick* angel." He really liked that word.

"So you've met her?"

"Not really. But it's like I said." With one hand, he waved a little flourish in the air. "She plays like an angel!"

"Kind of a weird instrument, though."

"That is what makes her a maverick."

When Dave Mizra left, Mr. Rodolfo gave up his tinkering and came to the front of the laundromat. I was tagging Dave Mizra's shirts, and when Mr. Rodolfo saw what I was doing, he shook his head.

According to him, Premium Service for Delicates was exclusively for women's wear. So when he read the tags, he said the same thing he had been saying ever since that article had been published in the *Chronicler*.

"Faggot."

Then he thumped back down into the basement.

15. What It Said in the *Chronicler* Article Taped to the Inside of Dave Mizra's Window

Indie Rocker Visits Local Shop

It's not every day an honest-to-goodness rock star stops by, but for David Ibrahim Mizra, custom jeweller and the owner of Mizra's Fire & Ice, that day was yesterday. The rocker in question? Veronica Heller, lead vocalist with indie rock darlings Wild Blue Bounce. The band will be playing a show at Foo Bar in July.

"I was just opening my shop when she walked right in," Mizra, 45, told the *Chronicler*. "I recognized her from photographs, but she was much taller than I thought."

The *Chronicler* earlier reported that Heller would be in the city's Evandale district to shoot material for a new video. In recent years, film and television crews have been drawn to the neighbourhood's gritty, inner-city atmosphere, not readily available in more gentrified boroughs north of Steinway Avenue.

"She told me she had heard that there was a famous jewellery designer in this area," Mizra said with a proud grin. "Of course she meant me."

When asked what the singer had purchased, Mizra was tight-lipped. "She was interested in many things, but all I will say is that perhaps you will see them soon at one of her concerts." Mizra also hinted that Heller wasn't the only celebrity to frequent his store. "Oh, yes," he added, "my shop is doing very well!"

Neither Ms. Heller nor her management were available for comment.

* * *

16. Nobody Gets Carded in Evandale

It took me all day to convince Nomi to sleep over at a friend's house. After that, I called the hospital to check on Mom. She was still sleeping. The person I spoke to told me not to worry, but this is why we have the expression "Easier said than done."

Later, when Calen pulled up in front of the Sit'N'Spin, he was surprised to see Nomi standing beside me.

"Thought you said she was sleeping over somewhere." He stepped out of the car and slung both arms flat across the roof, drumming his hands and bobbing his head. If anyone else did that, it would have looked dorky, but not Calen. He made it look natural. It was how his body worked (i.e., not like mine). He was one of those guys who can play any sport like a pro. Even car-roof drumming.

I explained that Nomi's friend lived in Rosemount, pretty near Toph's place, so we could drop her off on the way.

"I don't know." He poked a thumb at the back seat. "It's pretty tight in there. Like only room for one."

"Lemme quote you: 'Dude, your sister is. Like. *Tiny*.' Remember that?"

"I'm the third-tallest girl in my class," Nomi informed us.

In the passenger seat, Alana was listening. "Not a problem," she said through the window. "She can sit on my lap. There's tons of room."

It was true. Calen had this thing about skinny girls and Alana fit the bill. She was nearly as small as Nomi, but there was no mistaking her for a child. She was pretty, too, in a cheery-cherry-cheeks kind of way. She always looked like she was on the way to audition for a part in a movie in which the recurring motif was pixie dust.

"She'll fit no problem," she said.

Calen responded with a stern look. "Wait, it's not cool. We still hafta get—*you know what.*" He mimed drinking from a glass. "We thought we'd stop down here because we figured, well—nobody gets carded in Evandale, right?"

I didn't love that my best friend thought I lived in a place where alcohol flowed in lawless torrents through the streets, but I kept my mouth shut.

Alana laughed. "Not like in *Rosemount.* Before we drove down, Cal got carded—at three different places."

At least now I knew what was bothering Calen. He had failed to procure the requisite booze for tonight. You couldn't show up at Toph's without at least a six-pack.

"I don't get it," Calen said, genuinely pissed. "My brother even lent me his ID, which we all know he *never does,* and look." He pointed to his mouth. "I grew a moustache and everything."

I recognized this moustache. It was a pathetically wispy rip-off of the already pathetic one his brother wore around.

"I don't have to go to the Czerneckis', you know," Nomi

announced, sensing our hesitation. "Katie's not even my best friend anymore. It's *Jennifer* now. She's in grade four, *and* she plays the violin."

"That's nice, but you're staying at Katie's tonight, okay?" I helped-slash-pushed her into the front seat with Alana.

When we arrived at the liquor store, Calen eyed me nervously in the rear-view mirror.

"Don't worry," I reassured him. "It'll be cool." I hated to admit it, but he was right. Nobody gets carded in Evandale.

Except Calen.

When he came out again, we didn't need to see he was empty-handed to tell he'd been shot down. His expression did the job just fine.

"Yeah, so that didn't work out like I planned."

Alana snorted at him as he climbed back into the car. "It's the moustache."

Calen ignored her and turned to me. "You wanna try?"

"No way. They know me in there. I'm the kid who works at the laundromat."

Alana sighed. "I get carded buying rum balls. You'd have better luck sending Nomi in."

Calen's shoulders drooped. "You know any other places?"

I looked out the window, as if helpful ideas might be wandering around the parking lot. In fact, that's exactly what I saw. I pointed across to the rear of the Super Centre. "Take us over there. We can ask him."

Sitting against the wall was a thin man dressed for winter, even though it was the dead of July. He wore baggy camouflage pants, unlaced workboots and a hooded bomber jacket. He gestured wildly with his hands, as if he was in the middle of an argument with himself. Which he probably was.

"Dude," said Calen. "You realize that's a homeless guy."

"He's not homeless. He sleeps at the Emerson Centre, this rooming house near where I work." I bit my lip. "He's sort of a friend-of-a-friend."

"You *know* that guy?"

"Welcome to the neighbourhood," I said.

"Dude, that is messed up."

"Just drive over to him. I have an idea."

Calen turned around in his seat, looking at my sister. "Is he serious? You guys really know that guy?"

Nomi nodded. "It's B-Man."

17. You Can't Have a *B* without an *A*

Nobody knew what the *B* stood for. It was simply what everyone called him. Most of the time, B-Man stumbled around Evandale muttering to himself. All year long, no matter the season, he always dressed like it was Christmas. He was never without a hood pulled up over his head. When you put it all together—the stooping, stumbling gait; the bulging layers of clothes; the fur-fringed hood that kept his face in perpetual shadow—he looked less like a human being and more like a creature from under a bridge. If that wasn't enough to spook the locals, there was always Razor, B-Man's dog.

Razor was a big, meaty, chocolate-coloured mutt. By the looks of her, she had genes that ran the full range of *bull*—bulldog, pit bull, bull terrier. Needless to say, she came out looking fairly nasty. Despite the ferociousness of her face, however, it was the dog's other end you had to worry about. Razor was a *relentless* farter. The only person who didn't mind the stench, of course, was B-Man (probably because he reeked so bad himself).

"You sure about this?" Calen asked me.

We had parked close (but not too close) to the wall of the Super Centre where B-Man was pacing. Calen had cut the engine, but we just sat there.

"If you know that guy, go talk to him. Not me. Looks like if he breathed on you, you'd get AIDS."

Alana rewarded Calen's crack about AIDS with a slap to the back of his head.

"*Ow!*"

Sometimes, you can talk to B-Man and it's like talking to a regular person. There's a certain logic to the conversation, or something approaching logic. Other times—or rather, *most* of the time—it's gibberish.

I got out of the car and walked over to him. I had a feeling it was a gibberish day. B-Man was pacing back and forth, muttering to himself, Razor following at his heels.

"Solid ground. Fuckers always keep it shifting." At least that's what I think he said (apparently, but not necessarily, to his dog). "You find some solid ground, and you stick it." To demonstrate, he stabbed the air, fingers sharp as a blade. "Never know what's coming. The machine'll fuck ya every time. Cuz there's ghosts in there. Echoes! Wheels within wheels, man, wheels within wheels!"

"B-Man?"

He stopped and looked at me. Razor toddled over and sniffed my crotch. When I shoved her head away, she blasted out a fart.

"*Gross!*" was Alana's response, through the car window.

I stepped around the dog and the cloud of fumes. "B-Man? What's up?"

He didn't answer because he was too busy muttering to

himself. For a second, I thought it was a mistake coming over. Maybe I should have done what I usually did when I saw B-Man. *Ignore him.* Instead, I went a bit closer.

"I'm looking for A-Man. He around?"

B-Man paused for a second, then went on pacing.

"If you know where he is, could you tell me?"

More pacing. More muttering.

"B-Man? It's me, Kaz. From the Sit'N'Spin. I work for Mr. Rodolfo, remember?"

The moment I said "Mr. Rodolfo," B-Man flinched. I had his full attention. But instead of telling me where A-Man was, he charged at me.

Nomi yelled from the car. "Kazuo!"

I turned to run, but Razor already had a whiff of B-Man's rage. She was between me and the car, barking and farting for all she was worth. Before I could get away, B-Man grabbed hold of my T-shirt, pulling my face right inside the mouth of his hood. His breath in there was almost as bad as what spewed from Razor's ass crack.

"You tell John," B-Man said through gritted teeth, "that A-Man has the money."

"What are you talking about?" John was Mr. Rodolfo's first name.

"Money. From the poker."

I heard Calen start the car, and for a second, I thought he was about to bail on me. But he didn't. He gunned the engine and drove toward us. B-Man's eyes bugged out, and even Razor was shaken. She let out a skittish stream of little *putt-putt-putt* farts. Calen screeched to a halt and climbed out. He raised his hands to show B-Man they were empty.

"Hey, guy, we're not looking for any trouble, okay? Let go of my friend and we'll leave you alone."

He started to come around the car, but Razor growled at him. Meanwhile, instead of obeying Calen and letting go of me, B-Man re-tightened his grip on my T-shirt.

"Cool it, B," said a voice. "Kaz don't know the first thing about it."

It was A-Man, B-Man's only friend (no one knew what the *A* stood for, either). They were both ex-soldiers and they had served together in Afghanistan. Going over there shattered something in B-Man, or maybe he was already cracked to begin with. Anyway, neither one of them fared well after the big pullout. Now they both live full-time at the Emerson Centre.

A-Man strolled out from the far side of the Dumpsters, zipping his fly. He had been back there the whole time, taking a piss.

"I told you before," he said to B-Man. "It's all cool with me and Rodolfo. You gotta quit making such a big deal about it. Besides, I got 'til the end of the month to pay him."

"You do?" B-Man looked confused. It was possible he didn't know what month it was.

"It's really nothing." A-Man ambled over to us. Seeing the two of them side by side, you really got a sense of what opposites they were. B-Man was a short, squat, muscly white dude, while A-Man was tall, spidery and black. One thing they shared, however, was a penchant for headgear.

A-Man topped off his bald head with a kufi skull cap. It had once been white (I assume), but he wore it so often it was turning more the colour of—well, me. Kind of yellowy-brown.

"Let go of him, B. He's just a kid."

B-Man obeyed.

"What's going on?" A-Man asked me. He peered into Calen's Volkswagen.

I explained how we'd been shot down trying to buy beer for a party, and I thought maybe if we gave him the money, he could buy it for us. A-Man had a thick black goatee around his mouth. He rubbed it thoughtfully.

"Who's the kid?" he asked.

"That's my sister."

"Okay, well, it's not like I'm above buying booze for a minor, but c'mon—not *that* minor."

"Don't worry, she's not coming. We're dropping her off."

A-Man gave his goatee another rub. He had the sort of eyes that were always still, his lids always heavy and half-closed. It didn't give the impression he was bored or half-asleep; more that he was calmly considering something. He looked across the parking lot at the liquor store.

"Okay, I'll do it. But you have to understand that what you're asking me to do here is break the law. So I think some compensation is in order."

"Yeah," said B-Man, who had obviously caught on. "Twenty bucks!"

A-Man agreed. "Sounds about right."

"You mean twenty bucks for the beer, and then you guys keep the change?"

A-Man smiled at me like I was a child. "I mean you give me the money for whatever moonshine hooch you kids drink these days, and for the service of me buying it, you give B-Man and myself twenty bucks. Ten each, okay?"

I looked over at Calen. "You got ten extra bucks? I'll split it with you."

Calen shook his head. "He wants *twenty bucks?*"

"It's your fault," I told him. "You never should've grown a moustache. I mean, *tried to.*"

He sneered at me. "This was your idea. If you want to get this guy to shop for us, then you pay him. I'll pay for the beer, that's all."

"Tell you what," said A-Man. "We'll roll for it."

I knew this was coming.

Calen squinted at me. "What does he mean, 'roll for it'?"

"Dice," I said. "It's how A-Man decides everything."

"*Die,*" A-Man corrected. "It only takes one."

He turned to B-Man, who reached into a zippered pocket in his bomber jacket. His grubby hand came out with a little white cube.

"Put out your hand," A-Man told me.

I did, and B-Man dropped the die into the pit of my palm. I was surprised to see that the pips on each side weren't simply spots. Each one was a tiny black-and-white whorl, a yin-yang symbol.

"Whaddaya want?" A-Man asked. "Even or odd?"

"Odd."

"You got it. If you roll an odd number, you win. I'll buy you whatever poison you want for free. No surcharge. But you roll an *even* number, and it'll cost you the extra thirty."

"Wait, before you said twenty."

A-Man nodded slowly. "I did, but the machine craves balance."

"The *what?*" Calen asked.

I shrugged helplessly. "The machine."

It was A-Man's pet name for the whole universe. To him, we humble humans were nothing more significant than dust, falling between the gears. I think this was his way of making sense of the randomness of life, the fact that there doesn't seem to be any clear pattern to anything. But A-Man took the idea way too far. Basically, he didn't see the point of making rational decisions. Instead, he rolled a die.

"Balance?" I asked him. "Didn't you tell me once that the machine doesn't *want* anything, so why does it care about balance? *And*, how is it balanced if you suddenly charge us another ten bucks?"

A-Man considered this with his usual calm. "All machines crave balance. An unbalanced machine stops working." He tapped his chest with four long fingers. "I'm giving you something here: a chance. The original twenty was for the service, but now, by rolling for it, you get a fifty-fifty shot at beating the machine. To get something for free. That'll cost ten more. Total of thirty. Fifteen for me and fifteen for B."

I felt the twinge in my gut that always came from parting with hard-earned cash.

"Twenty-five," I said.

A-Man shook his head. "Just roll the die. Let the machine decide."

"Fine, whatever."

I crouched down (dangerously close to Razor's unpluggable sphincter). I sensed Calen and Alana, even Nomi, craning their necks to watch me. I wanted to put them out of their misery. I also wanted to stand up before Razor let one rip.

So I rolled.

18. Now for Those Next Two Letters (The Ones That Come after *A* and *B*)

Both of Topher Briggs's parents were wizards of finance at an uber-bank downtown. Accordingly, his family lived on Meadowlane Road, the wealthiest street in Rosemount. The house was a long bungalow-style mansion made of huge grey stones. A broad, U-shaped driveway curved around out front. By the time we dropped Nomi off and drove up to the house, it was already jammed with cars. We had to park three blocks over.

As we walked up, the music thumped through the windows, every one of which was blazing, flickering with the shadows of people. One of those silhouettes, I thought, was Christina Muñoz.

The inside of Topher's house was just as expansive (and expensive) as the outside. In the entrance, there were curved white walls, plants on pedestals and a grand, swirling staircase up to the second floor. The carpet was so thick you sunk an inch with every step.

I didn't recognize anyone.

We carried the beer into the kitchen, packed with more unfamiliar people. Suddenly, Alana squealed at a girl she knew. A second later, she vanished into the next room. Calen and I couldn't fit our beer into the fridge, so we left the box on the floor.

The door at the far end of the kitchen was cordoned off with masking tape. I recalled from earlier years that beyond that tape were the bedrooms, a big study full of books and a music room Topher's family called "the Salon."

Although Toph's parents turned a blind eye to his annual summer party, even doing him the favour of going away for the weekend, that masking tape was their one standing rule: that side of the house was off limits. This year, Toph seemed especially worried about trespassers.

Not only was there more tape than usual, there were tiny words written all over it. *KEEP OUT! FUCK OFF!* Or, for guests who had drunk themselves into a state of illiteracy, an easy-to-understand doodle of a skull and crossbones.

"*So*," I said to Calen as we opened the first of our warm beer, "you happen to see Christina on the way in?"

"Whoa, dude, we just got here. If you go looking for her right away, she'll think you're needy. Girls hate that."

Calen had a point. I tried to relax. This entailed leaning nonchalantly against the kitchen counter, beer clutched in one hand, my other one dangling down at my side, lamely patting my leg in time to the music. With the first pat, I hit something sharp. It was the corner of the CD Dave Mizra had given me that morning.

When I took it out, Calen gave me a weird look. "Dude. What's on the cover?"

"It's from the seventies," I said, as if that would explain everything.

"That a *ceeee-dee*?" someone asked from the kitchen table.

At first, I was just happy to see someone I recognized. Devon Whitney. He was sitting at the head of the table, his afro gathered back in a green headband, aptly embroidered with the word *SKILLZ*.

Devon didn't go to Rosemount, but I knew him from running track. He was one of the fastest kids in the city. Ever since high school started, he had consistently and authoritatively kicked my ass in the 400.

"Who listens to *ceeee-dees* anymore?" he mocked.

The other guys around the table laughed.

In my defence, I said, "A friend gave it to me."

Across from Devon was this older kid in a button-down shirt checkered like a picnic blanket and a pair of huge, black, thick-rimmed glasses. "That *Freudian Slap*?" he asked.

I wasn't sure if it was wise to admit this or deny it. "Uh … yeah?"

"*Stellar*. Shain Cope, right? Whoever your friend is, tell him he's got good taste. Lemme see."

I passed over the CD and the kid in the glasses nodded in appreciation. "Too bad he killed himself," he said at last.

"Shain Cope?"

"Yeah, I think so. He's dead, anyway. Happened in the eighties."

"I wouldn't know. The liner notes are in French."

"Kinda makes it a collector's item." The music geek handed it back—slowly, like he wasn't happy to part with it. Suddenly, he eyed me like an inquisitor. "You got a favourite song?"

I said the only title I remembered. "'Colt's-Tooth Blues'?"

The music geek approved. "*Stellar*. It's like he made up his own genre. It's fucked up, but it's good."

I nodded. Everybody was ogling the CD—and me, too. I didn't want to say anything to spoil it.

Even Devon had shifted his earlier verdict. "Sounds like it might be decent. Think maybe I need to hear this."

"Cool," I said. "I'll go put it on."

19. *Freudian Slap* by Shain Cope, 1978 (tracklist)

[1] Colt's-Tooth Blues

[2] Boat Riders and Mule Skinners

[3] Freudian Slap, Part 1

[4] There's A Girl On Murton Street (She Took the Ring But Won't Wear It)

[5] Punching the Guff

[6] Make A Man On His Merits

[7] Brickyard Jimmy (Kicks the Can)

[8] Splice the Mainbrace

[9] 50,000 Shares of Consolidated Copper

[10] Mr. Finneran's Mutt

[11] Freudian Slap, Part 2

[12] Get Me Home

20. How to Make a Roomful of People Shut Up and Stare at You Like You Just Morphed into a Manatee

In the living room, there was no sign of Christina Muñoz. In my fertile-slash-horny imagination, I hoped her absence meant she was out back, where Topher's patio included a massive swimming pool. My imagination also took the liberty of putting Christina in a red bikini. (It's the details that make all the difference.)

A bunch of people were sitting on the floor, lounging on cushions and rolled-up blankets. The stereo was embedded in the wall. A little tray poked out of it, propping up a pink iPhone stickered with fake diamonds.

A guy with an eyebrow ring lounged on the floor below it.

"You mind if I change this?" I asked him.

"Go ahead, s'not like I'm the DJ."

I put in the CD and switched the music. Nobody seemed to care.

I don't know what I was expecting to hear. The music Dave Mizra usually brought over was fast and upbeat, but this was different. This was a dirge, something you might hear at a funeral. It started with a piano, playing a sad, slow melody in a profoundly minor key. Here and there, the piano was complemented by a few plucks on something with strings, a cello maybe.

"This?" said the guy with the eyebrow ring. "This is what you wanted to put on?"

I nodded weakly and the music changed. It blossomed and swelled. It was still a funeral march, but it had gone from the burial of somebody old and decrepit to the death of an acrobat or a clown. Maybe the death of a whole circus. It was the same sad melody, only with trumpets and drums and a wheeze of accordions. That was when everyone in the room shut up. But it wasn't because of the music. No, everyone stared at me like I was a freak because of *the voice.*

Imagine a set of vocal cords pickled in whiskey for twenty years, then smoked over coals for another ten. Got that? Good. Now scrub them with sandpaper. That's Shain Cope. Imagine that voice—*singing.*

He heard there's rain in Paris
Gotta wonder if she's there
She always looked her prettiest
With drizzle in her hair
The sky's got nothing in it
Just the flapping of the crows
The sun's as bright as—

"What the hell?!"

Guess who it was, swearing at me from the patio doors. (A hint: she wasn't wearing a red bikini.) I hit the Stop button on the stereo and the room went horribly and embarrassingly silent. Meanwhile, Christina Muñoz was striding across the room and—even sans bikini— she looked *hot.* And, yes, I know they teach us that boys-slash-men aren't supposed to objectify women's bodies, and that makeup is a tool of oppression, and that high heels murder your calves, but when you see Christina Muñoz coming toward you, it's easy to forget everything Mr. Dearborn taught you in social studies.

"Who said you could touch my iPod?"

"It's yours?"

"Uh, *yes*."

"There was a guy in the kitchen. He told me to put this on."

"You always do what people tell you?"

"No. But … the guy had cool glasses."

Christina laughed, but not in the way I'd hoped. Not in a nice way. I don't think she got that it was a joke.

"His beard was pretty cool, too."

"Oh, I get it. You're high."

We were on track to set the record for Longest Conversation Ever with Christina Muñoz. Sadly, it wasn't going well.

"Actually, I'm not, I was just—"

"Okay, well, no offence, but whatever you put on just now? *It sucked.*"

"Oh."

"This what you were playing?" She grabbed the CD case out of my hand, squinted at it for a second and then said, *"Ew!"*

She jammed the case into my chest, pushed past me and put her iPhone back in charge of the music. She even scrolled back a couple songs, obviously to make sure we didn't miss anything.

"There, that's better."

"Uh, Christina?"

She responded with a *How-do-you-know-my-name?*-slash-*Have-you-been-stalking-me?* face.

"For a couple years, didn't we go to the same junior high?" I asked this like it had suddenly just occurred to me and, to add to the lameness of the question, I actually stuck out my arm as if to shake hands. "Nice to see you again."

Christina stared at my rigid palm like it was a disease. "You want to *shake my hand*?"

I went limp from the shoulder down. "No! I mean, we don't have to."

"I know we don't."

At this point, Devon Whitney came out of the kitchen, coolly inserting himself into the awkwardness of the conversation.

"Hey, babe," he said (not to me). "What's going on?"

Babe. Bold move.

"This guy put on, like, *music from hell.*"

Devon wagged his finger in my face. "Don't mess with a girl's music."

Thanks, Devon. Maybe you could've dropped that advice back in the kitchen. I was just about to say something to this effect when Devon Whitney did something appalling. Something *horrifying*. He put his arm around Christina's waist.

"'Specially my girl. She's fierce!"

"Your girl?"

"We hooked up this week." He said it like it was the easiest thing in the world. He didn't even bother to look at me as he spoke. He was gazing out through the big living room windows, the ones overlooking the patio. "Anybody in the pool yet?"

Christina nodded. "A couple people."

"Let's go, then. You brought your bikini, right?"

"Uh-huh," Christina told him, smiling as bright as a holiday in the tropics. "My red one."

21. Names with *Z*

So it turned out Devon Whitney was faster than me, both on and off the track. I didn't feel like moping back into the kitchen to tell Calen. So I decided to take a walk.

Out back, I deliberately ignored the people splashing in the pool. Topher's property was massive. There were several paths leading away from the patio. I chose one at random. It wound through a few curves between some hedges before leading to a small gazebo. A dim light under a metal shade hung down from the centre of the roof, giving off a gentle, smoky glow.

Someone sat alone on the bench. It was a girl in a red, pleated skirt, high-laced boots and a black camisole that showed off long, willowy arms. She had a book in her lap, so her head was cast down. Even still, I knew who she was by her hair: blonde, pink and purple dreadlocks.

"I know you," I blurted.

She looked up quickly, as if I'd startled her, and her eyes hardened. She looked tense. "You think? From where?"

I wanted to answer, but I couldn't. I was too struck by her face. Her face was gorgeous. She wasn't "hot," not like the girl I had just lost to Devon. This girl was more like movie-star gorgeous, the kind of face you don't believe exists, not in real life, and certainly not in a gazebo out behind Topher Briggs's house. But here she was.

"Hello?" She waved her hand. "You slow or something?"

"Sorry, what was the question again?"

She sighed, but her body remained rigid. *"From where?* Where is it you think you know me from?"

I put one foot on the bottom step of the gazebo. It creaked softly. I could see her face clearly now. Her skin was pale and her lips were thick, curved down slightly in the corners. It could have turned her face into a frown, or made it fish-like, but it did neither. It was because of her eyes. You barely noticed her mouth because her eyes were so bright. They caught so much light, everything else went dim.

"I saw you. I work at a laundromat on Steinway. The Sit'N'Spin. You walked past the window."

She seemed relieved. "Oh, yeah, I know that place. I play across the street sometimes."

"That's a crazy instrument you have."

She nodded vaguely. I expected her to elaborate, but she didn't. "What is it with grass?"

"Grass?"

"I was just thinking about it. Like, *why?* Why grass?"

"Are you talking about marijuana?"

She laughed. She threw her head back and let out one sharp whoop. *"HA!* Grass? Where are we, 1972? The least you could do is say *weed.* Or chronic. Ganja. Doobs. Skunk, kif, boom." The words sounded like sound effects in a video game. "Not even *my dad* says grass."

She closed her book and pointed over the railing, to the shadowy yard that stretched on forever. "I mean *actual* grass.

It's boring. Just look: you have this big house, you have all this property, you *obviously* have shitloads of money, and what do you do? You cover your property with the most boring plant in the world. " She took her beer off the railing and took a long swallow. "If I had a lawn—which I don't—but if I did, I'd plant something good. Something *interesting*. You ever seen a shell flower?"

I shook my head.

"They have these really long stems, all crowded with leaves like little green seashells. They remind me of the ocean—*and* they also happen to be good luck." She turned her shining eyes to me. "What would you plant?"

"Never thought about it." I took another step up the stairs. "But now that I am, I guess you're right. Grass *is* kind of boring."

"I hate *anything* boring."

"Venus flytraps," I said, with a certain authority.

She smiled. "*Definitely* not boring."

I was on the gazebo with her now. Her dreadlocks were tidier than I expected. There was style and precision to them, as if they were the work of a salon. Something about that surprised me.

"I like your hair," I told her, maybe to explain why I was staring.

She took one dyed-purple dread and held the tip in front of her face. "I have a confession to make."

"You do?"

"I know you, too."

"What do you mean?"

"It was you who just tried to put on some decent music for once. Aren't you?"

"Were you inside just now? I didn't see you."

"I was by the pool. I heard through the windows. I *love* Shain Cope."

I nodded, trying once again to appear knowledgeable. "He's great."

She frowned. "Too bad the skank made you turn it off."

I laughed.

"What's funny?"

"The skank. She's sort of the reason I came tonight. My friend told me she was single, and I thought—well, let's just say my friend was wrong."

For a second, she looked disappointed (or so I hoped). She shrugged, turning back to the boring grass. "Guess I can see why you'd like her."

With her head turned, I could take in her profile. The sharp line of her jaw, the smoothness of her forehead, the thin tendon that ran up the side of her neck.

"I'm not sure I do anymore," I said.

"Because she's taken?"

"No. I think I finally realized ... she's not for me."

"Here's what I know," she said, still gazing at the grass. "If you shaved that girl's head, she'd look *terrible*."

"Please don't tell me you *scalp* people over their choice of music."

She laughed. "No! I just think you can tell the most beautiful girls if you imagine them bald. If you can—and if they still look good—then yes, they're the real deal."

I tried to imagine Christina Muñoz without any hair. I couldn't.

"So ..." I said, not knowing where to go next. I thought about her playing across the street. "Do you know Dave Mizra?"

"Nope," she said, shrugging. "I asked him if it was okay to play my rattler on that corner and he said it was cool."

"Your rattler?"

"*The rood rattler.* That's what I call it."

"What's so rude about it?"

She laughed. "Not rude as in 'you forgot to say please.' I mean *rood.* R-o-o-d. It's a totally different word."

"What does it mean?"

"You know the giant cross they put up behind the altar in a church? That's called a *rood.*"

"I'm not really religious."

"Me neither. I just think it's a cool name and it fits, you know? Rood rattler. Just because of the shape."

A little pocket of silence fell between us. I went right up to the bench and leaned against the railing. Our legs were almost touching.

"Dave Mizra," I said. "The guy who runs the jewellery shop—he's really into your music."

When she heard this, she grinned. "He is?"

"He told me you were his angel."

"Angel?" She laughed, but not like before. This time it was a quiet, nervous laugh. "Trust me, I'm nothing like an angel."

You look like one to me, I thought. Which—unfortunately— is when Calen came crashing up the path, clomping right up on the gazebo with us.

"*Kaz! Dude!*" he panted. "What're you doing out here? I looked everywhere! You *goootta* come see this!"

"I was sort of in the middle of a conversation?"

Calen's eyes shifted to the girl on the bench. I could see him trying to make sense of her, trying to figure out who she was. "You guys neighbours in Evandale or something?"

The girl shook her head. "We just met."

"Okay, well, I'm sorry to interrupt, but this is serious." He grabbed hold of my arm. "You have to come see this. Like, *right now.*"

"See what?"

"Toph bet some guy a hundred bucks he could light a twelve-inch blue angel!"

I looked at the girl on the bench. "That's funny. We were just talking about angels."

She rolled her eyes at me, but in a nice way. She was smiling.

Calen didn't really care. "Are you coming or what?"

Still looking at the girl, I said, "You wanna?"

"Sure, why not." She stood up and linked her arm in mine.

Calen's face went all twisted. "Sorry, Topher said no girls."

Instantly, our arms came unhooked.

"I'll be right back," I told her. "I'm Kaz, by the way."

She looked at me intently. "Like K-A-Z?"

"Yeah."

"Cool. I start where you stop."

"What?"

"K-A-Z. All the best names have a *Z* in them."

"You think?"

"Of course," she said. "My name's Zoey."

22. The Inherent Danger of Placing an Open Flame between Your Legs

A blue angel describes the action of farting as hard as you can, while trying to light your ass-gas on fire. Just so we're clear on this. It also explains why the "angel" in question is blue. Ass-gas has methane and hydrogen in it, so the resulting flame would resemble (theoretically, and somewhat disturbingly) something you would cook with on a gas stove.

I say *theoretically* because truly robust blue angels are rare. When we were kids, Calen and I tried many times to light our farts on fire. Sometimes, we lied to each other for encouragement, claiming we saw a purplish flicker, a little cherubic spark, but more often than not, all we succeeded in doing was singeing our fingertips when the match burned down.

A *twelve-inch* blue angel? No, Calen and I were fairly certain that was impossible.

To get to Topher's room, you had to crawl under the spider's web of masking tape, the skulls, the crossbones, the KEEP OUTs and the FUCK OFFs.

His bedroom was a palace. Even crowded with a bunch of guys, you couldn't miss the king-sized bed, the massive flat-screen bolted to the wall, the separate cabinets for each of the

Big Three game consoles—along with a copy of every game you could think of. To top it all off, the end of the room was dominated by a huge aquarium full of monstrous tropical fish.

When we walked in, however, we didn't notice any of it. That's because Topher was sitting on the edge of his bed, dead drunk and naked from the waist down. He had his legs splayed wide with his unit lumped on the covers, pink and greasy.

"Shit," said Calen. "I don't need to see that!"

"He's really gonna do it," I said.

To my surprise, Becky was standing in the corner of the room.

"Hey, Kaz," she said, with a slightly subdued but still perky wave.

"I thought it was 'guys only,'" I said.

"You can't count Becky," Calen reminded me. "It's not like it's anything she hasn't seen before."

"A hundred bucks," someone said.

"You sure you wanna do this?" asked somebody else.

"Shut up," Topher told the room. He held up a Zippo lighter in one hand and a ruler in the other. He shut his eyes for a moment, and after a little concentration, he said, "Okay, I think I got one."

He lowered the ruler and the lighter between his legs and started trying to get a flame. The lighter sparked and sparked, and finally, after a bunch of tries, it lit up with a wavering yellow flame.

"I wouldn't do that if I were you."

The voice came from a girl, but it wasn't Becky. I turned around and there was Zoey.

"You'll blow your ass off," she said.

Topher was so startled he dropped the lighter.

"Shit-shit-shit-shit!" He scrambled to cover his exposed crotch with a pillow. *"What the fuck*?! I said no girls!"

"Yeah, I know," said Zoey, discreetly averting her eyes, "but I figured you wouldn't mind if I was saving your life."

Topher looked at her like she was crazy. "What are you talking about?"

"Think about it. If you light a gas on fire, you can be sure as shit—no pun intended—that it'll burn faster than you can contract your ass muscles."

"What does that even mean?"

"It means the flame'll sear right up your asshole and burn the shit out of you. Literally."

Topher sat there for a moment. "Really? Is that true?"

Zoey laughed at him. "There's one way to find out, but don't say I didn't warn you."

"You gonna do it, or what?" someone asked him. It was the guy with the eyebrow ring, from the living room floor. "If not, you owe me a hundred bucks."

"No way," said Topher. "I'm not paying."

"A bet's a bet," said Eyebrow Ring.

Topher ignored him. He glared at Zoey. "Nobody said you could come in here. I don't even know who you are."

"You don't know who half these people are," said Becky. "Neither do I."

"Shut up, Becks, I wasn't talking to you." His eyes were still on Zoey. "Who invited you?"

She shrugged. "Some guys I met."

"Who?"

"I don't know *their names.* They just invited me."

"You don't know who you came with?" Topher's eyes scanned up and down Zoey's body. "What's your name?"

"Zoey."

"Zoey what?"

She hesitated. "I don't have to tell you that."

"It's my fucking house. How do I know you're not, like, *a crazy person?*"

"Zamani," she said at last. "My name is Zoey Zamani."

"Zoey Zamani? Dumb name. Oh, and you owe my friend with the ring in his face a hundred bucks."

"Excuse me?"

"It's your fault I lost the bet, so you gotta pay."

"No way."

"I don't care, as long as I get my hundred bucks," said the kid with the eyebrow ring.

"You will," said Toph, "just as soon as—"

He stopped because he had been interrupted—*by his own ass.* Topher farted so long and hard it sounded like he was shitting a train. Everybody screamed. They plugged their noses and ran.

In a second, everyone was out in the hall and running for the kitchen. Zoey and I were pulled along with the crowd and, looking back through the door, I saw Topher plop down on the bed, as if all his energy had blown out, along with the monumental ass-monkey.

"Fuck," I heard him mutter. "I was saving that."

The last guy out of the room slammed the door and followed everyone else toward the kitchen. Someone pulled on my elbow. It was Zoey. Her fingers slid down my arm, and suddenly we were all alone, hand in hand.

"C'mon," she whispered, tugging me deeper down the forbidden hall. "You gotta see this."

23. *Clair de Lune*, Part 1

She pulled me along to the end of the hallway, to the Salon. It was a massive room with hardwood floors and a ceiling punctured with skylights. Through them, we could see the moon and the stars above us. In one corner was a huge, brilliantly white grand piano.

"Cool, huh?"

"You've already been in here?" I asked her.

She winked at me. "I like breaking the rules."

"It's so shiny," I said, staring at the piano. Even though my mother used to play one of these for a living, we only ever had a second-hand upright at home, back when Dad was alive.

Zoey circled around it. "Do you play?"

I admitted I used to, when I was younger. I told her my mom had once given me lessons but I was never very good.

"Too bad it's white. I'm a firm believer all pianos should be black."

"It looks good in the dark," I suggested. "Like a ghost."

Zoey didn't respond. She ran her fingers over the rim. Then, silently, she raised the fall.

"What should I play?"

"Nothing," I said. "Toph's mad enough already."

"I told you, I don't like rules."

She slipped her legs over the stool.

"Wait, don't."

She ignored me and looked up, her huge eyes catching the blue light of the moon. "I know just the thing."

I was about to run over and stop her, but I froze. Zoey had started playing *Clair de Lune*.

When I was a kid, whenever Mom tucked me into bed, she always went downstairs afterwards and played this song. She called it the perfect lullaby. It was one of the last songs she taught me (or tried to) before Dad died. I could never play it like this. It reminded me of something Mom used to tell me.

"A lot of people, especially people who don't play, think the loud pieces are the hardest. The fast pieces, the ones with a lot of jumps, lots of notes. They're hard in one way, but practice will always get you there. It's the slow pieces, the quiet pieces, the sad pieces that are really the trickiest. That's because there's always something you can't learn. You've just got to have it inside you."

It wasn't until then, standing in Toph's moonlit music room, that I understood. That thing my mother talked about—Zoey had it inside her.

"What the fuck?!"

Suddenly, the lights came on and I understood what Zoey meant about white pianos. At the flick of a switch, it went from a ghostly, mysterious gleam to looking like a cheap carnival ride.

"*What the fuck* are you doing in here?"

It was Topher. He was swaying in the doorway, his eyes wild (but at least he was wearing pants).

"Sorry," Zoey shrugged, going right on playing, giving up *Clair de Lune* for something random, just loose improvisation. "When I see a beautiful instrument, I just have to play it."

"Fuck that," Topher said. He was holding a wineglass full of beer and he pointed it at me. "So what, you two are like— *together?*"

"I just met her," I told him. "But you can at least be civil."

Topher laughed. "*Civil?* Who says '*civil*'? And like you'd know how to be civil to a girl. Becky told me all about you. She said when it comes to money, you're tight as a fish's ass."

Zoey snorted. "How civil of you to say."

Topher's face flushed red and he stormed over to the piano, slamming down the fall—*WHAM!* Zoey only *just* managed to pull her fingers out of the way. He could have broken every bone in her hands. Hell, he would have lopped off her fingers.

All I could think of to say was, "*Toph! Whoa-whoa-whoa-whoa-whoa!*"

"Shut up, Kaz! Take your slumdog girlfriend and—"

Before he could finish, Zoey screamed at him. "YOU FUCKER!"

She slapped the bottom of his wineglass. Beer and foam went everywhere. It sprayed on the wall, the floor—even inside the piano. Toph got drenched from the face on down.

"*Fffffuck!*" Topher shoved Zoey so hard she fell off the stool. He raised a fist in the air like he was going to hit her.

Which is when I (finally) stepped in. I grabbed his arm and he spun around, fists flying, and even though he was kacked up to the eyeballs, he still hit the mark.

Getting punched in the face comes with a very distinct sensation. First, all the pain shoots through your nose. It feels like your sinuses are wired to a car battery. Your eyes gush like you're sobbing (not the coolest thing that can happen to you at a party), and then the pain goes *bang* through your whole head and it's so bad it leaks into your legs, which of course morph into noodles.

My only salvation was the fact that Toph was extremely drunk when he hit me. The punch was on target but clumsy. For a second, I actually thought I might be okay, but when I took my hands away from my face, the room *really* started to spin—because it wasn't just tears and snot making my hands all slimy. It was blood.

Toph had given me one Big Daddy of a nosebleed. The awful redness dribbled through my fingers and turned the puddle of Toph's beer a vomitus pink.

The second I saw the red in my hands, all my most important organs floated away, drifting up through the skylights like lost balloons. Just as I collapsed on Toph's polished hardwood floor, all I could think was *I hope to shit I'm about to leave a big fucking stain.*

24. The Wisdom of Vomit

I felt like Shain Cope sounded, like the end of the world.

I woke up on Toph's front lawn. Calen and—here's a surprise—Devon Whitney were standing over me. They picked me up and, sagging between them like a damp laundry line, my shirt spattered with b-l-o-o-d (I was careful *not* to look down), I let them march-slash-drag me out to the car. Halfway there, my stomach voiced its sincere opposition to being moved. A searing mash of beer, bile and barbecue potato chips spewed out of me.

Devon nearly dropped me. *"Disgusting!"*

Calen, however, saw the wisdom of my vomit. "Yep, get it all out now. *One drop* in my car and you're walking home."

I heard voices behind me. It was Alana and—another surprise—Christina Muñoz. They were tagging along half a block behind us. I could hear Christina gushing about "the best reality show they've ever made." She was talking about *Big Daddy*.

When they heard the cough and splatter of my puke, they came running up to us.

"Are you okay?" Alana asked me.

"No, but my stomach feels better."

Christina winced at my shirt, now with a tasty new layer of abstract painting, courtesy of my gag reflex. "Sorry I got mad at you before," she said. "You have to admit, though. That wasn't the best music. Like, not for a party. Maybe not for anything." She giggled loudly. "Anyway, Topher is *such* an asshole. But seriously, are you okay?"

I wondered if she always jumped around like that from sentence to sentence. "I'll be fine," I told her. "I just need to get home and take a shower."

"Your girlfriend is crazy, by the way," said Devon.

"My who? She's not my—wait, where is she?"

"No one knows," said Calen. "After you passed out, she wanted to stick around, but Topher wasn't having it."

Devon laughed. "It took, like, *five guys* just to get her out of the house." He shook his head, recalling what I'd missed. "And I thought *my* girl was fierce."

Calen explained how supremely pissed Topher had been, how he said he was going to call the police, although he never did. He only wanted to scare off Zoey, who was screaming and kicking up a riot.

"Yeah," Devon repeated himself. "Your girl was *fierce*."

"She's not my girl."

"She is kind of hot," said Calen. "You got her number, right?"

"Oh, no! I didn't. I don't know anything about her."

"Not even her name?"

"Zoey," I said. "Zoey Zamani."

Alana smiled at me. "Cool name."

25. It Runs in the Family

I didn't sleep well that night. When you're lying alone in the dark, it's hard to ignore the lingering throb of a smashed face. But that wasn't the real reason. In truth, I couldn't stop thinking about Zoey.

In the morning, bleary-eyed, I did a Yellow Pages search for people named Zamani. There were forty-one listings, with addresses all across the city. I knew it would be stupid to dial at random. I recalled Calen's advice from the night before. *Girls hate needy.* Anyway, do people who play music in the street get their names listed in the phone book?

So I just sat there with a face like a junkyard, scanning up and down the addresses. I was still reading the list when a taxi rolled up out front. Through the window, I saw Mom ease herself out of the back seat.

After an attack, she prefers silence at home. For a day or so, she's kind of out of it, almost like she's still asleep. She hates it when Nomi bounces to the door, leaping up, hugging her, yapping like a puppy.

Mom's feet dragged up the stairs. The entranceway door

opened and closed. I heard a shuffling as she took off her shoes and pulled on her slippers.

"Kaz?"

"I'm here," I said, through the bedroom door. I didn't want her to see my face. "How're you feeling?"

"Tired. *Ironically*. Where's your sister?"

"She slept over at a friend's. Katie's mom'll bring her home this afternoon."

"I'm going to lie down for a while."

I waited, but I didn't hear the sound of her door. When I peeked into the hall, she was still standing there.

"The kraken wakes," she said dully. There was a weak smile on her face. I wasn't sure if she meant me or her.

"You okay?" I asked. "You want something to eat?"

"Not yet, first I'll—*Kaz, your face!*"

"Yep, I know. I was sort of there when it happened."

"When *what* happened?!"

"Just some guy I know. He punched me." I didn't tell her it was Topher. She might want to call his parents. That wouldn't be pretty.

"Punched you? *But why*?!"

I explained as much as I could, careful to leave out references to parties, girls, beer et cetera. There wasn't much left after the self-censorship. It was simply an argument that got out of hand.

"I should have been here," she croaked. "If I'd been with you, I would've—"

"Mom, stop it. Even if you weren't in hospital, it's not like I would have asked you to come along."

"But look at you!" She leaned forward, peering into my face.

My nose was about two inches too wide and purple blotches pooled under my eyes. "There was blood, wasn't there?"

I shrugged.

"Did you …?"

"Pass out? Of course."

Mom laughed sadly. "Passing out at the worst possible time. Runs in the family." She pulled me into one of those head hugs your mom gives you when she thinks you're still five.

"*Ow*! My face!"

I pushed her away and the nubs of bone in her shoulders jabbed my hands. They were way too pronounced.

"It looks worse than it is," I told her, unconvincingly. "I feel fine."

Mom shook her head. Her eyes were wet. "Later, we'll have Mr. Rodolfo lend us his car. We'll all drive up to Beauhaven. You let Tracey have a look at you for once. She'll fix us both up, you'll see."

26. Beauhaven

One knock-on effect of her illness is that Mom isn't allowed to have a driver's licence. So whenever we drive up to the Beauhaven Centre, it's always me behind the wheel. The centre is two hours away, in an almost-suburban town called West Olsten. As far as I know, there's no such place as *East* Olsten, but that doesn't seem to bother the people of West Olsten.

Never go there, by the way.

I'm sure there are a zillion places in the city—maybe even right in Evandale—where you can get retired hippies to ram-slash-dribble homeopathic smoothies down your throat, but if you asked Mom, nowhere was as good as Beauhaven.

As soon as you pull into the parking lot, everything looks false—the marble pillars (which are actually textured cement); the roof of wooden shingles (which are obviously plastic); the pair of potted evergreens on either side of the entrance (both of which are polyurethane Christmas trees). It's all synthetic crap, crafted to give the opposite impression: that Beauhaven is fully in touch with the all-natural world.

Out front is a sign painted with the Beauhaven logo. A

cartoon daisy, with the initials *BC*. Below it is the familiar slogan:

The Beauhaven Centre
Get Wellness!

(Mom had been trying for two years, but she hadn't gotten any yet.)

Tracey, the woman who ran Beauhaven, was a "reiki specialist." For Mom, this was crucial. Reiki came from Japan and so did she, at least in a roundabout way. According to her logic, if anything was going to work for her, it would come from her ancestral homeland.

"Please," I begged when we got there. "Don't make me go in."

"But Kaz, your face." Mom shook her head. "Nomi can't even *look* at you."

She was right. We had picked up my sister on the way and she was in the back seat—covering her eyes.

"I'm fine," I said. "Really."

"How would you know if you're fine? You're not a practitioner."

"What does that even mean? A 'practitioner'? If you'd said *doctor*, for once, then yes, you'd be right. I am not a doctor." I pointed at the Beauhaven building. "But neither is she!"

Mom shook her head. "I'm not hearing this. Tracey is wonderful—and you're seeing her."

"I am not." I turned and stared grimly out the window. The sky above Beauhaven was bright blue and completely empty except for a few fluffy clouds and a flock of big black birds. They looked ominous. And hungry. I willed them to swoop down and devour the place, but they weren't into it. They just flew away.

"You're going in," said Mom.

"Why can't you just go in and leave me here? I'll be fine!"

"Don't fight," Nomi told us, speaking blindly from the back seat. "It's bad for Mom if you fight. Stress is bad and then she'll—"

"I won't." Mom reached back to rub Nomi's knee.

"Well, he should do what you say." Nomi spoke as if I wasn't there. "He's supposed to know that stress is the problem."

"You're eight!" I told her. "You're not even supposed to *know* the word *stress.*"

"Your face is *gross,*" she retorted, which certainly shut me up.

Mom tugged down the passenger-side sun visor and flipped open the mirror for me to see. The bridge of my nose looked like a deformed potato and the two dark puddles under my eyes were swelling into lakes.

"Looks worse than this morning."

Mom smiled, vindicated. "Guess that means you're coming in with us."

(It did.)

Tracey was a thin blonde woman with faintly muscled arms. If you only saw her from behind, you might easily assume she was my age, a teenager—until she turned around, that is. Then you noticed the fake tan she used to hide her wrinkles and the sagging, scrotum-like skin around her armpits.

"Welcome back," she said to Mom, clearly happy to see her. "And who's this?"

"My son, Kaz. As you can see, he might be in need of some of your magic."

Why did she have to call it magic? All it did was highlight the obvious.

"What happened?" Tracey asked.

"He was punched," Mom said.

Tracey put her hands on her hips and regarded me with an almost obscene degree of sympathy. "Are you bullied at school?"

"It happened at a party," I said.

"We have counsellors here at the clinic."

"No, thank you."

"You realize it could be serious. If the bruising doesn't drain properly, there's always a danger of blood poisoning."

Great. Scare tactics. I began to feel faint.

"Oh, my goodness! You can hardly stand!"

Nomi shook her head. "It's what you said," she whispered. "Don't talk about blood."

Tracey nodded sagely and I sensed her writing "hemophobia" in a mental file.

"I'm fine," I said. "Seriously."

"Perhaps you could do something for him?" Mom said.

Tracey nodded. "Oh, certainly. We could fit you both into the large treatment room."

She led us into what looked like a regular doctor's office, only with two beds instead of one. Once Mom and I were lying on them, Tracey opened a drawer in one of the cabinets and took out what appeared to be a shiny, silver, carrot-shaped dildo.

"This," she said, holding it up, "is going to do both of you a lot of good."

I swear, I almost cracked up. "I don't think this is a treatment I need."

"Lie down," Mom told me. "You have to relax."

"How can I? What's she gonna do with *that*?"

"Your mother's right," Tracey said. She rested the weird-looking thing on her desk and lit a match. "Lie back, relax. You'll be fine."

She flipped open the fat end of the carrot-slash-dildo. It was hollow. She lit some short sticks of incense and dropped them inside. There were holes all over the surface, cut in the shapes of stars and crescents. Sweet-smelling smoke streamed out.

"What *is* that thing?" I asked her.

"A reiki wand," she said, as if it was the most common thing in the world. "Just relax, Kaz. You shouldn't speak while I treat you. It can interrupt the energy flow."

She loomed over me, eyes closed in concentration, swishing the suspicious instrument back and forth. In the end, that was all she did: wave her magic wand, filling the room with smoke. She didn't even touch us.

When the incense finally burnt out, Tracey stopped. "We'll give it twenty to thirty minutes to sink in," she said. Then she left.

"Now what?" I whispered.

Mom hushed me with a finger. "Do what she said. Relax. Let it sink in."

I tried to relax, I really did. Just as I was nodding off, I sat up, wide awake. I was angry.

"This is stupid."

"Kaz, lie down. This is the most important part."

"I can't do this."

"*Please*. It can't hurt."

"Are you paying for this?"

"It's worth it. It really is."

Suddenly, I was choking on the incense. "I need some air."

I jumped off the table and stomped out of the room, feeling like my suspicions about Beauhaven had been spectacularly confirmed. At the same time, however, I was mad at myself. A part of me had hoped everything Mom told me about this place was true. Maybe it would work. Maybe it was a miracle cure.

Unfortunately, that hopeful part of me had faded away, a bit like scented smoke, wafting through the holes in a magic dildo.

27. The Arbitrator

"What happened to you?" A-Man asked me, dropping a massive bag of towels on the counter.

"I got punched in the face."

"I've seen worse."

"You've been in a war."

A-Man didn't respond.

"Thanks again for buying us beer."

"Not a problem."

"Would've been even better if I hadn't rolled a two." I told him he could pick the towels up the next morning.

"One other thing," A-Man said. "When you see your boss again, tell him I might want to get in on another one of his poker games. I could use the, uh—y'know." He rubbed his thumb against his first two fingers.

"He's downstairs. If you want, you can tell him yourself."

A-Man considered this for a moment, leaning on the counter. Before he could make up his mind, we were both distracted by a dark shape in the front window. It was B-Man, glaring in at us.

A-Man shouted through the window. "Thought you were taking a walk, B!"

B-Man didn't say anything. He just stood there.

"Ignore him," said A-Man. "It's the best thing."

B-Man smacked the glass so hard, the whole pane shook. He raised his hand to do it again and I thought he might smash right through.

"Okay!" A-Man shouted at him. "Cool it, B, I'm coming."

He went out front, and in about three words' time, the two of them were arguing. With the washers and dryers going, I couldn't hear what they were saying. I did, however, hear the creak of the stairs behind me. Mr. Rodolfo was lumbering up.

"No-no-no-no!" He emerged from the stairs, waving his arms, and ran outside. He waggled both his index fingers in B-Man's face, swearing at him to get lost.

A-Man muscled between them, doing his best to keep the peace. It was quite a scene, but eventually, A-Man pulled B-Man away and Mr. Rodolfo came back inside.

"He comes around here again—the little one, I mean— you get rid of him. Understand?"

I nodded.

"If he won't listen, you got my permission to use the Arbitrator." He jabbed a thick finger into the shadows of the stairway, where it hung from two red, rubberized hooks, screwed into the wall. It was a massive crowbar. A long, heavy, kick-ass J of metal.

That was Mr. Rodolfo's Arbitrator. His own special way of settling disputes.

28. How Not to Take Out the Garbage

It was Saturday night, and as I mopped up at closing time, a few of the men from Mr. Rodolfo's poker night began to arrive. They rarely spoke to me. I figured that was because they were all men similar to the Brothers, men who had emigrated late in life and were therefore weak when it came to English. I thought A-Man might show up, but he didn't. Eventually, when all the poker players were safely ensconced in the basement, I flipped over the CLOSED sign.

The final thing on the to-do list was to empty the trash cans, haul the bags out back and toss them in the Dumpsters. Just as I stepped out the back door, however—

VVRRAAAWWWWN!

Some shithead in a black sports car came racing up the alley. He shaved it so close, his side mirror bumped one of the garbage bags. The plastic twisted around my finger and I thought it might be torn clean off.

"Fucker!" I yelled at him. You think he stopped? No way.

I was so pissed I dropped one garbage bag and threw the other one after him. But he had his foot down. The bag sailed through the air and came down with a *pop*. Right on the pavement. It burst open and melted into a puddle of candy wrappers, dryer lint and used Downy sheets. In the silence after the car was gone, just as I was putting the stuffing back into the bag, I heard music.

It was faint, far off, but I recognized the melody. It was Shain Cope. "Colt's-Tooth Blues." Maybe someone in one of the apartments was playing the song. I thought—*shit!* I had left the CD at Toph's! I'd completely forgotten about it, probably because I had left the party half-conscious. Sooner or later, Dave Mizra was going to want it back.

I stood there like an idiot, listening. There was something different about this version. It was Shain Cope's song, but not the one on the album. The piano intro had been replaced with something like a violin or a cello, and when the singing started, I was certain. It wasn't his voice. Shain Cope sounded almost demonic. This, on the other hand, was the voice of an angel.

29. A Ghostly Relic

Even with a whole building between us, I knew it was Zoey. Back in the laundromat, I switched off the lights. I didn't want her to see me. Not yet.

Through the front window, I saw her, right where I expected her to be, sitting on a bucket in front of Dave Mizra's place. She had her rood rattler propped against one shoulder like a double bass—which suddenly made sense. One half of the thing was wired like a harp, while down the centre strut, there were strings like a guitar. It was the second set of strings she was playing, with a long bow. She sliced it back and forth to produce slow, melodic groans, sounds that lay somewhere between a cello and a musical saw.

Her other hand manipulated the rest of the thing. She blew sad notes out of the horn fastened to the horizontal strut. She tapped at the junk swinging from the crossbar or pummelled the base against the pavement, *thumping* it to make sounds like an uprooted elm tree trying to dig itself back into the earth. It was the strangest one-girl band in the world, and on top of it all, she started singing:

You wish that she were still around
You wish that she were here
I thought I was a poet once
I'm just a profiteer
If only I were beautiful
Like something rotten on a beach
That stuff has got a kind of grace
Nobody ever sees

In the lamplight of Steinway, with Zoey's hair falling over half her face, the instrument looked like a ghostly relic, something dug up and reconstructed by a maniacal archeologist. It was a creepy scene, but it went perfectly with the music.

There weren't many people on the street, certainly no one standing near Zoey. Even the building ignored her. Dave Mizra's shop was locked up and dark (just like the Sit'N'Spin). However, I noticed a lone light, glowing in a window one floor up. A figure—it must have been Dave Mizra himself—was silhouetted behind the pale curtains.

Zoey must have known he was there, because every now and then, she glanced up at the window where he stood. It was like she wanted to make sure she had an audience, even if it was just one person. In truth, it was two.

She only played for another couple of minutes, not really keeping to the song, just riffing on the tune. Finally, without quite getting anywhere, she stopped. She stared down at the pavement, looking a little sad, and then began packing up her things. After that, taking me by surprise, she glanced across the street, right into the window where I stood in the dark.

It was too dark. She couldn't have seen me, but I took a

step backward anyway. She slung her big denim purse over one shoulder, hefted the instrument over the other and came across the street.

Seeing her headed straight for me, I panicked. I ran to the counter and ducked behind it. What would she think if she saw me? Standing in the dark, watching her? She'd think I was a creep.

I figured she would just walk past, but instead she stopped right in front of the window where I'd just been standing. Gently, she lowered her instrument and leaned it against the glass. *What was she doing?*

She took something out of her purse, something slim and shiny, and slipped it through the mail slot. It clattered on the floor. Then she walked off.

As soon as she was gone, I crept out of my hiding place. Lying on the tiles was the Shain Cope CD, the same one I had just been stressing about. Zoey must have rescued it before Toph threw her out of his house. I opened the door.

"Zoey!"

She was just about to cross over Emerson.

"Thanks for this!" I ran after her, waving the jewel case like a flag of surrender. "I really needed it back!"

"No problem." She looked past me, at the darkness of the shop. "Thought you were closed."

"I was, uh, downstairs."

Now that I was standing in front of her, I didn't know what to say.

"Your friend's an asshole, by the way," she informed me.

"Topher?"

"Who else?"

"He wasn't always that way. It's kind of a long-term project."

She let the instrument slide down her body and peered into my eyes. "How's your face?"

"Better than it was. You should've seen me a few days ago. Actually, no. Forget that. You *shouldn't* have."

"Did you hear me play just now?"

"Only a bit."

She smiled hopefully. "What did you think? Kind of a weird sound, huh?"

"I think it sounded amazing, like a whole band."

"Yeah, it's hard work. Makes me hungry. You know a good place to eat around here?"

"You ever been to What the Pho?"

"That's a restaurant?"

"Pho. Vietnamese soup."

"Never had it."

"Seriously? You should try."

"You wanna take me?"

"Oh. Yeah! Okay."

I turned to head up Steinway, but Zoey hesitated. "Will they let me in, you think? Most places don't like it when you show up with a giant cross—especially one with *bones* hanging off it."

"I could help you carry it home. If you live nearby."

She shook her head. "Our place is, like, *way* across town."

"Oh, okay." I was kind of hoping we were neighbours. "We could lean it on the wall outside. You'll be able to see it through the window."

Her eyes flashed. "Are you kidding? *No way.* I made this thing myself. It took *forever*. I gotta keep it safe. It's really important. To me, I mean." She took a step toward the laundromat. "Could I stash it in there?"

"My boss wouldn't like it."

"Not even for a little while?"

"I don't know …"

I looked up and saw the lights on in our apartment. We could certainly stash the rattler up there but: a) How would we hide it from Mom and Nomi? b) Both of them would probably want to meet Zoey, which would be weird and, of course, c) I was basically ashamed of where I lived.

"But you're closed," Zoey said, citing the obvious. "Your boss isn't even there."

"Actually, he's downstairs." I explained a bit about his poker nights, how on Saturdays, a bunch of guys came by and played cards for money.

"As long as he knows that's illegal."

"What is?"

"Um, *organized gambling*? For money? In a place of business?" She shook her head. "*Totally* not allowed."

"Is it just me, or is that a weird thing to know?"

She shrugged. "So can I stash it in your work or not? Otherwise, I'm going home."

"If he found it, my boss would go crazy. He saw you outside once and he thinks you're … well, 'a freak.' His words, not mine."

"What docs he know? I've not even met the guy."

"It's just the way he is."

"If we come back and get it later, he'll never know."

"I don't know …"

"Okay, whatever." She hefted the instrument onto her

shoulder again. "You wanna keep your job, I get it. I'll see you around."

"Wait."

"Yeah?"

"If we're really, *really* quiet, we can hide it in with the dry cleaning."

30. What the Pho?

What the Pho had much the same layout as the Sit'N'Spin, except instead of washers and dryers, there were tables and chairs. It was a long, narrow strip of a room, with a big window up front and an open kitchen in the rear. The place was decorated with old posters that looked like they had been stolen (not without violence) from a defunct travel agency. Two flat-screen TVs were bolted to the walls, running a perpetual loop of Asian soap operas.

Zoey thought the place was cool, but had no idea what to order, so I requested a basic bowl of pho for us both.

"How come it's so red?" she asked, poking the meat with her chopsticks.

"It's rare beef."

"Is that even legal?"

"You've eaten sushi, right?"

"Yeah, but that's fish."

"And it's raw. But it's good, right? This is just rare."

"Rare." She poked it again. "I think that's worse."

I looked around the restaurant. "Do any of these people look sick to you?"

"He does." She pointed to a stooped wreck of a guy, staring at the televisions.

"That's not sick, that's just … *old*."

She returned her attention to the bowl. "Okay, so what's this?"

"Tendon. A little chewy, but good."

"Do you always take girls here? I'm not sure it's a good idea."

"For a girl who plays music in the street, you're not very adventurous."

This comment was greeted with silence.

"Just try some," I said. "Trust me."

She did.

"Wow," she said. (Vindication!) "Why have I never had this before?"

"Questions I can't answer."

We started eating. I took the opportunity to stare at her mouth. Watching her slurp and chew like that—what can I say? It made me want to kiss her.

Halfway to the bottom of the bowl, she asked, "Why does your boss hate me so much?"

The mention of Mr. Rodolfo brought me back to the real world. "He has a narrow definition of what it means to be 'normal.'"

"Ick."

"I know."

We went on eating in silence for a while. On the TV in the corner, it looked like a Chinese soap, dubbed into Vietnamese. You didn't need to speak either language to see the words didn't match the actors' lips.

"Do you come here because you're Vietnamese?" she asked

me. "I don't know much about Vietnam—*obviously*—but you look like you might be."

"I'm not, but don't worry, nobody gets it right. I'm half Japanese, but my dad was black. He was from Barbados, originally. He died of a heart attack, about three years ago."

"Oh, no."

"I'm okay with it now, but it's not the sort of thing you ever really get over. It bothers my sister more than me, makes her worry about my mom."

"I guess between us, we've got one full set of parents."

For some reason, I was surprised. "Did something happen to your mom?"

"She's okay, but she ran off with some guy last year. Not that I can blame her. My dad can be a bit like your boss sometimes—cyc-ce, *an asshole*."

I asked her what her asshole dad thought of her playing music in the street. She said he didn't like her practising at home and besides, she could take care of herself. It felt good to be learning about her, like she was giving up her secrets, just for me. I wanted more of them.

"What about school? Will you be going to Evandale in the fall?"

She shrugged as if it didn't really matter. "I don't know. Maybe. If we stay in town."

"You're not staying?"

"Depends on my dad's work. He, um, teaches courses at Falconer. My favourite one's called Philosophy of Music. It's pretty cool, but right now it's mostly evenings and weekends. What we really need is for him to get tenure, for once. That means a full-time gig."

"I hope he gets one. Then you'll stick around, right?"

"Maybe," she said, looking away.

I didn't like the way she seemed distracted. I wanted to say something to grab her attention. "You know what I thought, the first time I saw you? When you first walked past the window where I work?"

Her attention returned, but not the way I wanted. She was squinty-eyed and suspicious. "What did you think?"

"These are the exact words. I thought, 'Holy shit, it's Jesus!'"

She laughed. "Shut up."

"I couldn't see your face and—well, look what you were carrying."

"Wait, so the guy who runs the jewellery store says I'm an angel—and you thought I was *Jesus*? That's a shitload of divinity to pile on a girl."

"It's true."

She smiled at me, but only with half her mouth. "You have a weird way of giving compliments."

"How do *you* give a compliment?"

She laughed.

"Go ahead," I said. "I can take it."

"You think I'm gonna pay you a compliment, just cuz you asked for one?"

I stood up, spread my arms and spun in a circle. "Look carefully. I'm sure you can find something worth at least *a little* praise."

She covered her face, obviously embarrassed. "Stop spinning like an idiot!"

I did.

"Okay," she said. "I got one."

Before she could tell me what it was, a dog barked outside the window. Only it wasn't just barking, and it wasn't just any dog. It was Razor and she was going berserk. She raced past the window, and a moment later, B-Man went scampering after her.

"Oh, crap."

"Who was that?" Zoey asked.

"B-Man."

"You *know* that guy?"

"We should go," I said. "Like right now."

"*Why?*"

"Because I think I know where they're going."

31. How to Detect a Lean-In Moment

Razor leapt up at the Sit'N'Spin's huge window. B-Man struggled to keep her from crashing through it. Inside, a crowd of Mr. Rodolfo's poker players taunted the beast, shooing it with the backs of their hands, snarling at it from behind the safety of the glass. A-Man was there, too, out in front, trying to pull B-Man toward Emerson. He must have shown up late for the poker game.

"Shit." I stopped halfway up the block and grabbed Zoey's arm. "We should wait here."

"*I can't!*" There was real panic in her voice. "I need the rattler!"

She tried to pull away but I held on tight. I slid my hand down her arm and we were holding hands, unintentionally, just like at Toph's party.

"It's okay. I hid it pretty good. They won't find it."

She spun around and glared at me. "You don't understand. I can't go home without it. *I need it.*"

"We'll get it. We just have to wait."

Mr. Rodolfo came out of the Sit'N'Spin. He had the Arbitrator. He started hollering, pointing the hooked end of the huge crowbar in B-Man's face. Behind him, the Brothers stood watching, arms folded, grim and silent as ever.

A-Man got between them, grabbing hold of the Arbitrator. He was trying to keep the peace, but it was hard to say if it was working.

"Is that him?" Zoey asked me.

"My boss? Yeah."

"He really *is* an asshole. What is that thing?"

"He calls it 'the Arbitrator.'"

Zoey scoffed. "You need a new job."

"He pays me pretty good."

"I'll *bet* he does."

I squinted at her. "What's that supposed to mean?"

"Look at him. He looks like a *Sopranos* reject."

It was true. The Arbitrator was huge, but in Mr. Rodolfo's hands, it looked more like a chopstick. I tried to explain to Zoey that just because you spoke with a slightly thick-tongued accent and carried a wrecking bar into the street to defend your business, it didn't make you a mobster.

"He's just a regular guy," I told her.

Zoey let out a derisive shot of laughter—*HA!*—and covered her mouth. "Oh, my god. I just realized! He's not even trying to hide it. It's a freakin' *laundromat!*"

"So?"

"You do realize there's more than one meaning for the word *launder*, right?"

"Um, no." But then it dawned on me (vaguely). I had an inkling that the term was used to describe a process of hiding stolen money. "You mean, like, *money laundering?*"

"*Exactly.* Let's say—hypothetically—you stole a shitload of money. If you didn't want anyone to find out, you'd hafta disguise where it came from. Basically, there're two ways to do that. One, you start a business and pretend it makes more money than it really does. Say, for instance, a laundromat. Or two, let's say the money was stolen direct from a bank. Then it'd have serial numbers. The police and insurance companies can trace those pretty easily. That's why you have to mix up the numbers, exchange the money that you stole for new bills, and send the old ones off in all different directions. Basically, you wash the money. You launder it." She pointed to the crowd of men. "Spreading it around in a gambling game is one way to do it."

"Wait, you're saying Mr. Rodolfo *robbed a bank*?"

"How should I know?"

"Why do you even know all that, about money laundering?"

"Don't you watch television? Every cop show for like a hundred years has had a money-laundering episode. It's like a ... like a *trope*."

"That's TV, not real life."

But the seed had been planted. I thought about how protective Mr. Rodolfo was of his office in the basement. I thought about how the doors down there were always locked. I thought about the way the Brothers barely spoke to anyone and, even though I had gotten used to it, how eerie and threatening that silence had been at the beginning of high school, when I first started working for Mr. Rodolfo. I thought about how obsessed he was with keeping everything "good for business."

"No way," I said, in spite of all that thinking. "I'm telling you, he's just a regular guy."

"Who threatens people with a—what did you call it? 'The Arbitrator'?" Her fingers made a pair of mocking air quotes.

"That's just how he is."

A-Man was finally getting the situation under control. He was pushing B-Man back to the corner of Emerson. Razor was still barking, still leaping up on her hind legs, still yanking against her collar. Nevertheless, A-Man calmly guided them both away.

B-Man's interruption had put an unofficial end to Mr. Rodolfo's poker night. A couple of the men inside came out and got into cars. Eventually, the only ones left were the Brothers and Mr. Rodolfo himself. They chatted for a while in low voices, before finally locking up.

Once they were gone, I snuck up the street and let myself in. The instrument was just where I had left it, untouched.

"Well, that was fun," Zoey said, when I brought it out to her.

"Can I help you carry it home?"

"I don't live around here. I better catch a streetcar." She glanced up the street, where one was already on its way toward us. "Usually, they gimme shit for bringing my instrument on board, but at this time of night, they don't care so much."

I was disappointed, of course.

"So," I said, "you really think my boss is a gangster?"

"He sure looks like one."

I laughed. "I guess he does."

"Thanks for dinner, anyway. It was good."

"No problem. Maybe you could leave the instrument at home next time. It'll make life easier if we didn't hafta stash it somewhere every time we want to hang out. I mean, if you feel like hanging out again."

"You're cute," she said.

"What? Why?"

She tapped the side of her head. "You're always thinking ahead. I like that."

This was unexpected. "I am?"

She nodded. "And you're honest. You say what you feel."

"Is that my compliment?"

She smiled. "Maybe."

There are moments in life when you should lean in—i.e., quit talking and kiss the gorgeous girl standing right in front of you. Detecting these moments is a skill. I was crap at it. Zoey, however, knew what she was doing. As the streetcar rumbled through the intersection, drowning out our words, she tipped forward and pecked me on the cheek.

"Gotta go."

"Wait, can I call you? You have a phone, right?"

She scooped a random paper out of her purse and scribbled the number.

"Bye," I said, as the doors of the streetcar flapped open.

"I'll see you soon."

She lugged the instrument up the steps and our first date (if you want to call it that) was over.

32. DeWinter Hills

From what Mom tells me, when Nomi was born, I was dead jealous. Here was this precious blob that sucked up every drop of my parents' attention. I was eight years old, not at all accustomed to sharing.

One day, maybe to prove to me I was still wanted, Dad came home with a basketball. It was a green and white one, printed with the Celtics logo, a little leprechaun leaning on a stick. I loved it in spite of being tragically inept at any sport involving equipment—especially a ball. I could run and I could swim, but throwing? Catching? Kicking? I was useless.

It was the same with a basketball: I sucked.

I went out on the driveway, where I bounced it too high. I jammed my fingers. I tripped over my feet. Three dribbles and the ball stubbed off my toe and went bounding into the street. I rallied after it, of course—like an idiot—and I probably would have died that day if Mom hadn't yelled at me through the window.

"Kazuo!"

She was just in time. This sleek, black nuclear sub of a

luxury car torpedoed around the corner, right between me and the ball. Mom came running out with the little Nomi-blob balled up in one arm. She was furious, but all she did was hug me with her one free hand.

"You *have* to be more careful."

I just stared at her.

"Promise!"

I nodded.

After that, Dad started taking me to this park in Rosemount called DeWinter Hills. There weren't any hills there and I had no idea who Johnny or Jenny DeWinter was. All I knew is that off in one corner, there were three pristine basketball courts.

"This is a game of *misdirection*," Dad explained to me the first day. "You know what that means?"

No, I didn't. I was, like, *eight*.

"You pretend to do one thing, while you're really doing something else." That was how Dad summed up basketball: an exercise in fakery.

"All you have to do is be able to fake—a pass, a shot, just a step with your foot—and *POW!*" He dribbled straight for me, faked a shot, then twisted past for an easy hoop. "See what I mean?"

I did. Dad was never the most athletic guy in the world. He was short, stocky, with pudgy cheeks and a bit of a gut. But he had strong legs and dextrous arms, and these—along with a good fake—got around me every time. (Also, did I mention I was eight?)

It took me a couple years to master the art of shutting him down. I remember clearly, just after my eleventh birthday, the first time I stuffed him. He was as surprised as I was.

"I think you're getting the hang of this," he panted afterwards, a massive grin on his face.

I improved even more. It wasn't long before I could flat outrun him. I guess I started to get bored with it. Calen and Topher and some of the other guys from the neighbourhood played pickup and (for once in my life, thanks to Dad) I was decent enough to join them. We'd stopped going down to DeWinter Hills by then, but occasionally we still did.

"Now," he said, after a long hiatus of not playing with him, "let's see if you still remember what I taught you."

"Maybe I'll teach *you* something."

I was up twenty to nothing when Dad sucked in a screeching breath and, in this slow, horrifying collapse, went down on his knees.

"Dad! What is it?!"

He couldn't even answer me. He just coughed and waggled his head like he needed to shake something loose.

"Dad!"

"I'm okay," he sputtered. "Just dizzy." He smiled at me. "You're really good."

I didn't believe him. I just watched limply as he climbed back to his feet. As soon as he got there, he slapped the ball out of my useless arm and, only using his right hand, dribbled up the court for a layup.

All the way home, he kept saying, "I'm fine. I was only faking. Remember? What did I teach you? That's what it's all about. Misdirection."

I wanted to believe him. It was just a fake, just something he pulled so he wouldn't get shut out. I didn't tell Mom about what happened, and a week after we played, Dad was dead.

33. Dave Mizra's Secret

The next night, Calen, Alana and I wanted to see a movie. Before we could go, I had to put in a shift at the Sit'N'Spin. Midway through the afternoon, it started to rain, so when Dave Mizra came jogging across the street, he held a plastic bag over his head. It did little to keep him dry.

"Just some shirts today." He piled three damp, button-down Oxfords on the counter. I was surprised there were so few. He often did ten at a time.

I brought up the pad of Premium Service receipts.

"Actually, no thank you. Just regular today."

"Regular dry cleaning?"

This wasn't the Dave Mizra I knew. He looked worn out. Maybe it was only the rain, his fine black hair dripping down to narrow his face, but he definitely looked thinner.

"Are you sure?" I asked him. "Not Premium?"

He didn't answer the question. He just asked, "How much for your regular service?"

"You mean when *I* do it? You pay by the pound." I picked up the shirts, mentally weighing them. "This won't cost much."

"Good. Let's do that."

"Really?" It seemed odd that the guy running the most successful business on the block suddenly wanted by-the-pound laundry service instead of Premium Service. "Doesn't seem like you."

"Cutting back. You know how it is."

"But you're Dave Mizra."

He laughed, but it didn't end right. The sound trailed off and he stared at me for a long time, as if he genuinely needed to be reminded who he was. Then, taking me completely by surprise, his eyes welled up and he started to cry.

"Whoa-whoa-whoa, are you okay?"

He shook his head, because (obviously) he wasn't. He covered his face with both hands.

"You want some water?" I ran to the bathroom on the far side of the dry-cleaning booth and filled a glass from the faucet.

"Did something bad happen?"

He didn't say anything for a while, just dabbed his face. "I have some troubles."

"You do?" I always thought of Dave Mizra as the cheeriest guy in Evandale.

"My wife," he said. "In our home, near Algiers. She was in a car accident."

"Oh, no. Is she okay?"

"She's fine."

"Injured?"

He shook his head and spread his arms wide. "Completely unharmed."

"Wait, so what's the problem?"

"Because of the other man in the accident. He is an important businessman from our town. It's a lot of trouble for us. He intends to press charges—even though this accident, it was all his fault. Now my wife is going to court; the papers have been filed; and because of this, she will not be allowed to come until the case is settled. It's a great delay, and if something goes wrong, she may no longer be able to come at all." His eyes went glossy again. "It's not right for a man and wife to be apart so long!" I thought of how often Mr. Rodolfo called this man a faggot. How stupid was that? Obviously, Dave Mizra was crazy about his wife. "The man from the accident, he is asking for a bribe. It's blackmail."

To me, the solution was simple. "Pay him off and get it over with. If it'll get your wife here, just pay the guy."

He threw up his hands. *"How?!"*

"Wire the money."

"What money?"

"Duh!" I pointed across the street. "The money you make over there."

Dave Mizra shook his head. "I make nothing," he said.

"No way." I almost laughed in his face. "Famous people come to your shop. Veronica Heller, even."

Dave looked out the window for a while, not saying anything. "It was a lie," he whispered.

"What?"

"The Wild Blue Bounce. I don't even know them. The music sounds like whining to me. No spirit. But I know this is what's popular nowadays, so ..." He shrugged like he was weighing a grapefruit in the produce section. "So I chose her."

"What do you mean, you 'chose' her?"

"I made up that story. She never came to my shop. You really think someone like that would come to this neighbourhood? Why do you think there were no pictures? Don't you think I would have taken pictures? I told the man at the *Chronicler* she was 'a private person' and he believed me. *Ha!* Journalists."

"You mean she never came?"

"Does it matter? No one reads this newspaper, the *Chronicler*."

"So what are you going to do?"

"Perhaps I'll have to sell the shop. I think I should become a lawyer. They make all the money. A doctor, perhaps." He laughed when he said that, but it was all wrong again. It was the kind of laughter that made you think of being alone.

34. How to Kiss a Homeless Girl

Calen was giving me the *you've-morphed-into-a-manatee* look.
"I can't believe you kissed a homeless girl."

"Just a peck on the cheek. Not like it was a big deal."

"Except she's homeless."

"She's *not* homeless."

Calen and I were sitting in the café around the corner from the Metro Valley Cineplex, waiting for Alana to show up. We were going to see *Sudden Conquest*.

Most kids from Rosemount, kids like Topher, with rich parents, talked about how they were going to grow up and make kick-ass investments or start the next Facebook.

That's what I liked about Calen. He didn't care about any of that stuff. It suited me fine because I was too poor to have an opinion. Calen was different. He genuinely liked cars, girls and baseball. He had always liked cars, girls and baseball. He was the sort of person old people from the fifties meant when they said "straight shooter."

Which is also why he thought it was strange for someone to play music on the street.

"I'm telling you, she's not homeless. Her dad teaches philosophy at Falconer."

"Have you actually *seen* her home?"

"No."

"So she *might* be homeless."

"She's not."

For a moment, Calen gave this some serious thought. "Maybe. I guess. She was kind of too hot to be homeless."

I smiled. "Exactly."

"If she's not homeless, you should call her," Calen advised, suddenly changing his tune. "It'll be cool, like a double date."

"You think? I just saw her last night. What happened to *needy*?"

Calen shook his head at me like I was an infant with a spilled bowl of mushy peaches. "That only applies *at the beginning*. You guys've already kissed, so that stage is over. Now you'll *screw it up* if you don't call."

I took out the piece of the paper where Zoey had written her number. As I unfolded it, I was surprised to see a familiar symbol. A daisy with the initials *BC*. It was a flyer from Beauhaven, complete with its familiar slogan: *Get Wellness!*

"That's weird."

"What?" Calen craned his neck to look at the paper.

"My mom goes here."

"So?"

"It's, like, *way* out of town."

"So?"

"I don't know."

"Whatever. Just go call her."

I went outside and dialled the number.

"Hello?"

"Hi, is this Zoey?"

I heard music in the background, the carnival-at-the-end-of-the-world melody of "Colt's-Tooth Blues." It was rapidly becoming our theme song.

The music stopped. "Who is this?"

Before I could tell her again, a man with a deep voice grunted something I couldn't hear.

"I'm on the phone!" Zoey yelled back at him. "What is it?!"

"I said," the man hollered, "don't switch it off! Listen to it again!" That must have been Zoey's father. His voice was gruff and aggressive. He was slurring his words. He sounded drunk.

"And I said, *I am on the phone!*"

The music came on again, but at a lower volume.

"Sorry," Zoey whispered. "Who do you want to talk to?"

"*You.* It's me, Kaz. I took you for pho, remember?"

"*Kaz!* What's going on?"

"I wanted to see what you were doing."

She lowered her voice again. "Not much."

I told her where we were, that we were headed for a movie. She said she wouldn't mind getting out of the house for a while.

"Who're you talking to?" the man demanded.

"A friend of mine," Zoey answered.

He laughed, but not in a nice way.

"Shut up," Zoey told him.

I wondered what Mom would do if I ever told her to shut up.

"You're not going anywhere," her father told her. "You've got work to do."

"If this isn't a good time," I said, "we could always—"

"No. It's fine."

Zoey's father said something else in the background, but I couldn't understand it.

"I know it already!" Zoey shouted at him.

There was a clatter of noise that might have been plates cracking or maybe a crescendo of percussion in the Shain Cope song. Then more crashes and bangs—definitely not any kind of music. Suddenly, Zoey's voice was right inside my head, a ragged whisper.

"Save me a seat. I'll be there soon."

35. Zoey Buys a Coffee

When Zoey walked in, she was like a completely different person. Gone were the cut-off jeans, the torn tights, the killer boots, the off-the-shoulder T-shirt. She was now in a patterned, dark-green skirt; simple black tights; brown suede boots, low-heeled and low-cut; and a white button-up top that hugged her chest in a way you couldn't ignore (at least I couldn't). Her dreadlocks, instead of exploding out in all directions, were fastened back in a prim ponytail.

Her makeup was different, too. No more bruise-black eyeshadow and matching lipstick. Now her face was blushing the colours of peaches and plums. If you had never seen her before, you'd take her for a preppy.

"Is that the same girl?" Alana whispered to me.

I nodded.

"I take it all back," Calen said. "*Definitely* not homeless."

Zoey waved at me and came straight over. She stood at the table and bent to kiss me on the cheek—as if it were something she did all the time.

Calen jumped out of his seat and pointed at her.

"You're Zoey, right?"

"Yep." Zoey nodded and gave him a blank look. "You're Kaz's friend?"

"Uh … we met at Toph's, remember?" He sounded disappointed she didn't remember him.

Zoey smiled politely. "There were a ton of people there. What's your name again?"

"Calen."

Alana cleared her throat. "And I'm Alana," she said, followed by a dramatic pause. "His girlfriend."

"Nice to meet you."

"So, uh, what school do you go to?"

"Actually, I'm home-schooled. My dad knows a ton of stuff. He teaches at—"

"Falconer," Alana finished. "Kaz told us."

Zoey scanned the big chalkboard mounted behind the counter. "You guys mind if I grab a coffee? I've been working all day."

Working? I thought. I couldn't tell if she meant it ironically. Did standing on a corner strumming and thumping a weird instrument count as work?

"Sure," Alana said, looking at her watch. "Calen and I'll go get seats. We'll meet you there."

"We will?" Calen asked. He was obviously curious about Zoey.

"Yes," Alana said sternly. "We will." She dragged him away, but not before giving me a wink, one that meant, *we'll leave you two alone …*

Zoey had wandered over to the counter, where she ordered a small regular coffee, the cheapest drink on the menu. She paid, turned to leave, but then stopped.

"Excuse me," she said to the guy behind the counter, a pimply kid no older than me.

"Yes?" He raised his eyebrows hopefully, grateful for Zoey's attention.

"Can you break a twenty?"

"Sure!"

Zoey handed him a twenty dollar bill. "How 'bout a ten, a five and five ones. Okay?"

She took the change but she didn't put it away. Instead, she counted the bills out on the countertop, laying them down one by one. Then she stared at the money, thinking.

"Oh, my god!" she said. "I'm so stupid!"

It wasn't only her clothes that had changed; her voice had shifted, as well. It was faster and higher pitched. She sounded like she was doing an impression of Christina Muñoz.

"I forgot my dad dumped all these ones on me when I left the house. I totally need to get rid of them. They're so annoying, don't you think?"

"Totally."

I sort of felt sorry for the kid behind the counter. Maybe he didn't get much attention from girls, what with his skin being a bit messed up. I also wondered what Zoey was doing. If I didn't know better, I might have thought she was flirting—which made me wonder about her taste in men. If she flirted with guys like him, what did it say about me?

"Oh, wait! I know!" Zoey picked the stack of bills off the counter. "I can put all my ones together, then you can give me a ten, yeah?" She laid a stack of ones on the counter.

The kid gave her a ten from the register.

"Great, thanks! You really helped me out." She turned to leave, but the kid stopped her.

"Wait," he said. "You're short one dollar. There's only nine here."

"Really? Lemme see." She reached out and I noticed her nails were painted to match her face, the orangish-pink of early autumn.

She took the bills from the cashier guy and counted them onto the counter.

"Oh, my god! You're right!" Her voice went even higher and she giggled like a baby. "I am *sooo* sorry. No wonder they have you working cash. You're smart."

"Hey, thanks."

"Okay, here. I have a few more ones left from my dad. Why don't I give you a ten and a one—that makes eleven—and with the nine ones I gave you, it makes twenty. I'll put it altogether and then I can get my original twenty back, okay?" She giggled again. "God, I'm *so indecisive!*"

The kid smiled at her. "I'm sorry to say it, but you kind of are."

He should have done that more often. You didn't notice his skin so much when he smiled. The till was still open so he handed back her original twenty and took the pile of change from her.

Zoey shook her head. "All that for nothing! I'm such a ditz sometimes."

"We better go," I said to her. "The movie'll be starting."

As soon as we were outside, Zoey's voice went back to normal. *Weird.* Had she really been flirting with that guy? We passed a trash can on the way and Zoey tossed in the cup of coffee she had just bought.

"Hey! You didn't even drink that."

She shrugged. "I changed my mind. I wasn't kidding about

being indecisive. One moment I want something, the next I don't." She looked toward the cinema. "Anyway, they probably have a rule about outside drinks."

It made sense, but only kind of. Why would she take all that time to buy a coffee she wasn't going to drink? It bugged me all through the movie.

It wasn't until the very end that I figured it out.

36. Sudden Conquest

The movie was shit. I have no idea how we ended up picking it. It was basically a submarine war movie. In space. The good guys drove a space-sub called the *Conquest* (hence the title). That was about all the information you needed before the explosions started. Most of the time, I like explosions in a movie theatre, but not *just explosions*. That's what this felt like.

When we hit explosion gazillion-and-two, my brain turned to fermented bean curd. Or rather, *it wandered*. I kept thinking back to what Zoey pulled with that clerk in the coffee shop. In the middle of the big, spine-cracking meta-explosion of a climax, I figured it out.

I leaned over to her, my lips right at her ear. "If you needed ten bucks, you could've just asked me."

Her body went rigid. "What're you talking about?"

"What you pulled on that guy in the café. It was cool. You totally conned him out of ten bucks, didn't you?"

She let go of my hand.

"Zoey?"

She didn't answer.

"Seriously, I thought it was cool. That guy was an *idiot*."

Zoey made a hasty grab for her purse and stepped over Calen and Alana to get to the aisle. Calen didn't get it. In his world, you watched a movie to the end. Always.

"You can't go now. There's, like, five minutes left!"

I followed her out, but Zoey wasn't in the lobby. She was down on the sidewalk, standing near the road. I went out to meet her.

"What're you doing?"

"It's called flagging a taxi."

"But why?"

Several blocks down, something alarmingly taxi-like crept toward us.

"What's the big deal?" I said. "It's only ten bucks. It's not like I'm gonna call the cops."

"Shut up!"

"What's your problem?"

"Just leave me alone. I'm going home, okay? I changed my mind. It's a dumb movie."

"I don't get you."

"What's to get? You hardly know me."

"Exactly! Why do you think I wanted you to come?"

She turned again and looked for the taxi. It was stuck at a red light. Seeing her like that, turned away, willfully ignoring me, I realized she was right—I hardly knew her. I wanted to change that. A part of me wanted to know *why* she had pulled that thing in the coffee shop, but another part of me didn't care, and both were tiny compared to the biggest part of all: the part of me that just wanted her to stay.

"Okay, so maybe you feel guilty about what you did. Maybe you needed the money and you were too embarrassed to ask me to lend you some. Believe me, I know what that's like. Needing money." I thought I was getting through to her, but she was still staring at the taxi. "I thought it was a cool trick. It reminded me of something my dad used to say, about faking somebody out in basketball. That's what it was like and—seriously, what's ten bucks? The guy behind the counter was an idiot and you conned him. It's not a huge deal."

"Stop saying that!"

"Saying what?"

"That I *conned* him. You're wrong. I just ripped him off, that's all." She looked down. "It was just stealing."

"Looked like a con to me."

"That's cuz you don't know what it means. Haven't you heard that old saying? 'You can't con an honest man.' It's true. The clerk was an idiot, but he was an *honest* idiot. He was just doing his job."

Zoey raised her hand for the cab, but I grabbed it to stop her. "Okay, fine. You *stole* some money. Ten bucks, I don't care. I told you—I *totally* know what it's like to need some extra cash. It doesn't mean you have to go home already."

"Actually, it probably does."

"*Why?*"

The light was green now and the taxi was on its way.

"I liked it when you thought I was divine," she said. "Nice to get mistaken for a goddess, or an angel, or whatever. Something heavenly, anyway. But then, when you whispered to me in the movie, it felt like I'd lost all that."

"You haven't. It's still true."

"Honest?"

I nodded. The cab pulled to the curb.

"No one's ever figured it out before," Zoey admitted.

"So?"

"Guess it means you're smarter than most. Apart from my dad, most guys in my life have been pretty thick."

"You think I'm smarter than most?"

"You are today."

We stared at each other for a second. Neither of us was angry or confused anymore. Strange how fast it melted away.

"You pull that sort of thing a lot?" I asked her.

"My dad says, when you see an opportunity, take it."

I took a step closer to her, but the cab driver whirred down his window. "You guys need a ride or what?"

"Hold on."

In my head, there had been a kiss coming. A real one. It was a lean-in moment—and I missed it (of course). Because Calen came dashing out of the cinema.

"Hey! The movie's over! You guys coming back?"

"No," I told him, in probably the boldest move of my life. "Zoey's not feeling well. I'm gonna take her home."

She flinched. "You are?"

"If you're okay with that."

She bit her lip. "Actually, yeah, okay. My dad's away tonight."

The driver looked relieved when, like a perfect gentleman, I opened the door for Zoey, and then climbed in beside her.

37. What Zoey Did

Like I said, it took me nearly the whole of a crap movie to figure out what Zoey had done. It all came down to how she had deliberately laid her money on the counter in front of the guy, instead of giving him the cash directly. That was how she did it.

Usually, when you ask for change it's a two-sided process: One side (in this case, Zoey) hands in a bill and the other side (the cash register, basically) spits back the same amount in smaller denominations. Simple. Which is why Zoey complicated it—by adding a *third side* to the equation: the countertop in between. She used the counter in order to confuse the guy and make him introduce an extra ten bucks into the mix (which she inevitably ended up with).

It went like this:

He Said / She Said	Zoe's Cash	Countertop's Cash	Cashier's Cash	All Is Revealed
Zoey: Can you break a twenty? Cashier: Sure! Zoey: How about a ten, a five and five ones?	$1 $1 $1 $1 $1 $20 ___ $25	Nothing (expect maybe old coffee stains)	$1 $1 $1 $1 $1 $5 $10 $10 ___ $30	She starts with $25, but keeps the one dollar bills in her bag, so there's a total of $55 in play. Now keep an eye on those ten $1 bills ...
Zoey: Oh, wait, I'm so stupid! My dad dumped all these ones on me!	$1 $1 $1 $1 $1 ___ $5	$10 $5 $1 $1 $1 $1 $1 ___ $20	$10 $20 ___ $30	Instead of putting the change in her bag, she lays it out on the counter. She picks up only the $10 and the $5, leaving the $1s in the middle— and then she introduces five new $1 bills.
Zoey: I know, I can put all my ones together then you can give me a ten.	$1 $1 $1 $1 $1 $5 $10 ___ $20	$1 $1 $1 $1 $1 ___ $5	$10 $20 ___ $30	She now has $20 in her hand, but on the counter there's $5 in ones, which at this point belong to her.
Cashier: Wait, you're short one dollar.	$1 $5 $10 $10 ___ $26	$1 $1 $1 $1 $1 $1 $1 $1 $1 ___ $9	$20 $20	She only adds four $1s to the five on the counter, so when she gets $10 in return, she's up by $1 to $26. At this point, she owes him just $1. If she hands it over, they're even. But that's not what she does ...

He Said / She Said	Zoe's Cash	Countertop's Cash	Cashier's Cash	All Is Revealed
Zoey: Oh, my god, you're right! Okay, here's a ten and a one. That makes eleven and you can give me my twenty back. God, I'm such a ditz!	$5 $10 $15	$1 $1 $1 $1 $1 $1 $1 $1 $1 $1 $10 $20	$20 $20	Except she's definitely not a ditz, and here's where the trick happens. Those ten $1 bills in the middle? They now belong to the cashier, not to Zoey. Because they're on the counter, he can't see that. So when Zoey adds $11 to bring it up to $20, she's only giving him $10, but receiving $20 in return.
Zoey: All that for nothing! I'm such a ditz sometimes!	$5 $10 $20 $35	Back to nothing but coffee stains.	$1 $1 $1 $1 $1 $1 $1 $1 $1 $1 $10 $20	Despite what Zoey said, all that wasn't for nothing. It was for $10. She walks in with $25 and walks out with $35 (plus a coffee she didn't even drink).

38. Val Mer Residences

We made out in the back of the cab. Zoey's skin felt smoother and thinner than anything I'd ever touched. Or maybe it was just my imagination, an illusion of contrast, the way the roughness of her dreads brushed the backs of my hands when I slid my fingers behind her ears. I expected to taste the lime-and-mango fruitiness of lip gloss (something like what Becky had worn), but Zoey smelled of something simpler, like hot bathwater or a glass of milk.

We were nearing the east end of the city, where the buildings were more derelict and the streets emptier.

"Where are we?"

She shrugged, a little embarrassed. "This is my neighbourhood."

Vacant buildings stood like forgotten monuments. "Seems like a weird place to live."

"Not everybody has a grand piano in the living room, you know."

"That's not what I meant. I mean, why so far east? Falconer's on the other side of the city. It doesn't seem very convenient, like for your dad."

"Oh, yeah, well, we started out with this pretty nice place, an apartment on campus, but ..." Zoey bowed her head and rifled through her giant denim purse. I thought she would come up with photographs or something, but she just kept rifling. "Turned out there was a problem with vermin. Bugs or rats or something. The whole building was fumigated, so they were like, 'come out here and take your pick.' I think Falconer owns the land. They're planning to build another college or something."

"Out here?"

"I guess." Zoey stopped rifling and closed her purse. "How come you're so interested in the landscape?"

"Just seems weird is all."

When I turned away from the window, Zoey's face was right there. Her big eyes were electric in the flash and flow of the street lights.

Then we were making out again—in the back of a taxi, in the gloomy shadows of warehouses and metalworks, rushing past the shipping ports of an endless black lake. It all seemed appropriate and (this may sound strange) kind of romantic.

After a couple turnoffs, we arrived at Val Mer Residences, a two-storey apartment block that nearly had a view of the lake, if it wasn't for the massive sugar refinery standing in the way. The apartments were two buildings connected in an L-shape. They sprouted from one corner of a fenced-in sandlot that might have once been the bud of a residential development but had failed to blossom.

Half the *L* wasn't finished yet. It was just a naked shell, surrounded by scaffolds, wheelbarrows and piles of gravel. I could see that the construction had been left unfinished for a long time. The wood was beginning to buckle, leaving everything slumped and crooked. Zoey led me toward the completed side of the building (thankfully).

"I think it's kind of charming," she said.

"You do?"

"Sometimes you gotta *look* for what's beautiful; it's not right there on the surface." She shrugged. "Beautiful means different things to different people."

I thought of how Becky and my boss had thought Zoey was a freak when they first saw her, but how I thought something entirely different.

"Don't worry," Zoey told me. "It's nicer on the inside."

39. Water from a Fisherman

What do you think was in my head as Zoey tugged me down the corridor toward her apartment? Making out some more? Her eyes? Her hair? A blow job? Sex? What she was wearing? What she was wearing *underneath* what she was wearing? Nope. None of that. I was thinking about Mr. Dearborn, my *ex* health-class teacher.

Let me explain.

From the moment I started at Evandale, Mr. Dearborn was my favourite teacher. He could do anything: math, English, chemistry, social studies. Basically, he was just good at putting stuff in your head—and making it stick there. He believed people who were too into one subject cared more about information. True teachers, he said—people who could teach anything—they were more interested in knowledge. *All knowledge.*

Dearborn had this saying: "Information gets you through a test, but it's knowledge that gets you through life." You might think this sounds sensible. It might even sound like common sense. Ironically, however, this was precisely the idea that got Dearborn fired.

Evandale High had a *Three Strikes and You're Out* policy. I'm not sure what baseball has to do with good behaviour, but people think it sounds good, so they use it. I never expected them to use it on a teacher.

Mr. Dearborn's three strikes went like this:

1. The Amy Handler Bad Word Incident

This happened when Mr. Dearborn judged the school's annual short story contest. He awarded the grand prize to Amy for this story about two sisters driving up to a cottage and then fighting over a boy. The problem was the thing was full—*brimming*—with novel examples of the worst profanities you can think of.

There was some debate over whether or not Amy was deliberately trying to piss off Mr. Dearborn, but most people thought no, it was an honest story. All the details were there. The way the older sister walked as if she was in heels, even in Birkenstocks; how it felt to do a face plant on the surface of a lake; how it felt to have your heart broken. (Plus, everybody knew that over the previous summer, Amy's sister had stolen her boyfriend.)

After the contest, Amy was supposed to read the story in front of the school, but she only got through two paragraphs before they switched off the mic. Afterwards, Mr. Dearborn made his famous speech. "To a writer, there's no such thing as a bad word. Each one has a time, a place, a feeling. Taking words away from a writer is like taking wood from a carpenter, taking water from a fisherman. To a writer, the only *bad* words are the ones that aren't true."

(Strike number one.)

2. The 17.3 Incident

This happened in a social studies class called World Issues. Dearborn informed us that the average age at which a human being loses his or her virginity is 17.3. It wasn't like he was encouraging us to go out and start screwing; he was merely quoting the results of an extensive and reliable study. You can just imagine the volcanoes going off at the next PTA meeting. As for me, I had no problem with the statistic. I was proud to know that if you counted Becky—dubious, yes, but *if* you counted her—I was nearly nine months ahead of the curve.

(Strike number two.)

3. Boys' Eleventh Grade Sex Ed Incident

With all this in mind, you have to wonder what they were thinking when they assigned Dearborn to teach two weeks of boys' eleventh grade Sex Ed.

"Boys," he said, when his two weeks were almost up, "I'm beginning to fear I'm not doing you justice. Some of these are the same videos they showed me when I was your age. So I know from experience that when it came to some of the really crucial stuff, very little of it helped." He opened his briefcase. "Yes, *of course* it's important to know which direction an egg travels down a fallopian tube, but let's face it, unless you've got your heart set on becoming a gynaecologist, a good deal of what you really need to know happens ... *on the outside*. Which is why I brought this in."

He held up a DVD.

It was porn.

Well, it was and it wasn't. Technically, yes, it was pornography in that it was a film of two people having sex, but there were no beefy, glowing-orange men and the woman didn't have fake tits-ass-eyes-nails et cetera.

What Dearborn brought in was different. The film had been produced in Montreal by a group of regular people who were honestly trying to make what they called "educational erotica." They were *definitely not* porn stars. (The guy looked a bit like a shaved rat and the woman's breasts were floppily genuine.)

"Let's try to be mature about this," Mr. Dearborn told us before he popped in the DVD. "There's a lot more to sex than rolling a condom on a banana."

I know he was trying to do us some sort of weird favour, but think about it: watching porn with your chemistry-slash-English teacher, while he makes it *even more* squirm-inducing by standing beside the screen, offering helpful commentary like:

"See what he's doing there? *Foreplay!* Highly recommended."

Or:

"*Lube.* It's not just for after school, when you lock yourself in the bathroom."

Or:

"Notice how he holds the base of his penis to slide it in. It's like a lot of things in life: without a bit of guidance, you can end up anywhere."

Yeah, I thought, *already learned that one the hard way.* So yes, it was—without a doubt—the most awkward thing that had ever happened, but somewhere behind all the wincing and squirming, I was thinking what I'm sure a lot of us were thinking.

Best.
Class.
Ever.
(Also: strike number three.)

40. Bottom Drawer

Zoey unlocked the door to her apartment while I tried to remember everything Dearborn had taught me.

Inside, I expected shelves full of her father's books, hefty bricks about philosophy and music theory. There weren't any. There weren't even any bookshelves. The only furniture was a TV on a nightstand, two caved-in recliners and a kitchen table with mismatched wooden chairs. The nearest thing to literature was a stack of *Sports Illustrated*s on the floor beside the TV.

Zoey went into the kitchen and opened a cupboard. I saw that inside, there were only bottles, one each of vodka, rum and Irish whiskey.

"What are you staring at?"

"It's not what I expected."

"What did you expect?"

"I don't know. Something different."

She led me over to the fridge, where she took out a bottle of Coke, followed by a fifth of Captain Morgan spiced rum from the cupboard beside it. When the fridge door thunked shut,

I spotted a magnet printed with a familiar symbol. A cartoon daisy with the exclamatory words *Get Wellness!*

"Beauhaven," I said, tapping the magnet. "My mom goes there."

"Really? My dad, too. He's deep into the whole health-food, working-out thing. The diet's okay, but I'm not into getting stabbed with needles."

"Stabbed?"

"Acupuncture. My dad says it 'keeps him sharp,' which is his idea of a joke." She poured us rum-and-Cokes in huge red tumblers. "If you're gonna stab me with a needle, I better be getting a vaccination or a tattoo."

"Do you have any?"

"Tattoos? Just one."

"Where?"

"Maybe I'll let you have a peek and maybe I won't. First, tell me what you expected to see when you came in here."

"More books, I guess."

She laughed. "Why would you think—*oh!* I get it. You mean like because of my dad. The professor. He keeps all that stuff at his office at the college. Here, hold these." She handed me the two cups and then picked up the bottles. "Lemme give you the grand tour."

There was a hall off the entrance that led to a couple bedrooms and a bathroom.

"That's my dad's," Zoey told me, as we passed a murky room, the door open only a crack.

Zoey's bedroom was as sparsely furnished as the rest of the apartment, but it seemed more alive, more lived-in, than the other rooms. The bed was unmade; clothes were all over the floor; newspaper clippings and pictures from magazines were pinned over a small desk. A torn poster for Wild Blue Bounce covered one of the walls, Veronica Heller standing front and centre.

I was about to sit on the stool by the desk, when Zoey stopped me.

"That'll wreck your back. Just sit on the bed."

I wanted her to join me, but instead, she reclined on some pillows on the floor. The big red cup sat in the valley of her stomach.

We talked. I told her about my dad, what he was like and how he died. She told me about her mom leaving because she didn't dig her dad's lifestyle. Moving all the time, college to college to university, trying to nail down a decent teaching gig. Her mom couldn't take it.

I wanted to tell Zoey about Mom's illness, but I didn't. I had vowed I wouldn't tell people, and I stuck to it. (Well, sort of. Apart from the people I'd already told.) All I said was that my mom had once been a musician, but that she lost her job and now she worked in a library. It was what I told most people.

"She'll go back to the orchestra eventually."

"That why you work all the time? For the mobster?"

"No, we get money from my dad's life insurance. My mom's pretty practical when she wants to be. She didn't take the lump sum, so we get regular cheques. Oh, and I already told you. He's not a mobster. He's just a guy with a dry-cleaning business."

"That's what they all say."

"I work there because I'm saving up."

"For what?"

"For school."

Zoey rolled her eyes. "*Boring.*"

"What? Why?"

"Everybody and their pet llama saves for school. It's like a cult. Why doesn't anybody save up for something *interesting*?"

"Like a lawn full of Venus flytraps?"

"At least it's interesting."

"How're you supposed to get a good job if you don't—"

"Look up *boring* in the dictionary, you'll find a picture of a good job." Something about the way she said this made her sound older. To top it off, she drained her glass (while I was only halfway to the bottom of mine). I felt insulted, partly because she had just told me I was boring, partly because she had this older voice she could call up whenever she wanted, and partly because she was a better drinker than me.

"How much?" she asked me suddenly.

"What?"

"How much have you saved?"

I wanted to impress her. "A little over ten thousand dollars."

She lowered the glass from her lips. "Not bad."

"My last girlfriend dumped me because she said I was cheap. Maybe, but c'mon, that's a lot of cash, right?"

"I can't believe you saved all that working at a laundromat."

I had achieved my goal; I'd impressed her. I took a big, bold gulp of my drink, stupidly forgetting it wasn't just Coke. Halfway down, the burn of rum made me gag. I spat it out in a foamy gush—all over the bed, all over the floor, all over me.

"*Kaz! What the hell?!*"

"Sorry! I'll clean it up!" I jumped to my feet but I had no idea where to go.

Zoey grabbed a ratty sweater off the floor and started

mopping. She did the floor, the bed and finally me. She dabbed at my chest. My stomach. My belt …

"Is that cola-puke on your crotch, or are you just glad to see me?"

It was painfully obvious what was happening. I say *painfully* because it's true. (Getting a boner in a pair of skinny jeans isn't the easiest thing in the world.) Zoey's dabbing morphed into—well, let's call it more of a rub. Her hands were gentler than Becky's. Something I appreciated.

"Wait," she said, once my jeans were around my knees. "I've got something for you."

My head was spinning. "Like *a gift*? Right now?"

She pushed me toward the closet. "In there."

I stumbled out of my pants and opened the doors. Inside was an old armoire.

"Bottom drawer," Zoey said.

As I reached down, I thought: *condoms. This girl thinks of everything!* But when I pulled open the drawer, I saw something else.

A gun.

A big black revolver, lying on top of folded clothes.

"Fuck," I whispered.

"Yep," said Zoey, her older voice returning. "That's one way to put it."

A million ideas flooded my head (like a fizzy spew of rum and Coke). A gun? For what? Why did she want to give it to me? I remembered how her dad had sounded on the phone. Angry, maybe even violent. Wasn't there a movie like this? Some dumb kid gets a blow job in return for killing a guy? Is that what Zoey wanted me to do? Kill her father?

(Needless to say, propositions of murder make for a *serious* boner-kill.)

I cradled the gun on the flat of my palm like a dead budgie. "I have no idea what this means," I said, turning around, "but I think you've made a mistake here becau—"

I stopped mid-sentence because Zoey was practically naked. She was lying on the bed in her underwear (the famous pink leopard-print bra, with panties to match). It would have been the sexiest thing that had ever happened to me, if only the universe hadn't introduced *a big fucking gun* into the equation.

Zoey sat up. "What the hell?! Put that down!"

I did. It made a deep, echoing *THUNK* on the wood of the armoire, then rocked back and forth.

"You're not wearing any clothes," I said stupidly.

"Yeah, I sorta noticed. I didn't think you'd turn around with a *fucking gun*."

"I didn't think you wanted to show me one!"

"I didn't!"

She blushed all over and scrambled into a T-shirt.

"Then why was it just sitting in—"

"It's not even mine!" She stomped over and stuffed the gun back into the drawer. "It's my dad's."

"He carries a gun?"

"No, of course not. He's not here. If he *carried a gun*, he'd have it with him now, wherever he is. He just keeps it in the house."

"What does he need a gun for?"

Zoey pointed out the window. "Maybe you haven't noticed, but it's not like we live in the best neighbourhood."

Even worse than mine, I thought.

"He puts it in my dresser sometimes," she explained. "Like when he leaves me alone for a night. But then he doesn't tell me where, or which drawer. He's an idiot."

"Wait, so why did you want to give it to me? If it's your dad's?"

"Not the gun, stupid. I meant *those*." She pointed to the back of the drawer, where a box of condoms peeked out from under a folded sweater.

I'd been right, I just hadn't seen them. *Stupid!* But maybe there was still a chance …

"So, um … you think …?"

Zoey shook her head. "I'd say the moment passed. But don't worry, I'm more pissed at my dad than you."

The gun seemed to bother Zoey in a deeper, more complicated way than it bothered me. I was freaked out, but as long as it stayed out of sight from then on, I was fine. For Zoey, though, I sensed there was a bigger picture she didn't want to tell me about.

She went back to the bed, her body slumped like the empty skeleton that made up the building's other half.

"You should go home."

I tried to accept this. "Yeah, well, I gotta open up the laundromat tomorrow, so …"

"So you better get going."

I told her to text me if she was in the neighbourhood. Maybe we could hang out again. She said she would, but I wasn't sure if she meant it.

Out on the street, waiting for the streetcar to take me back in the opposite direction, I thought: *I bet that gun will be the craziest thing I see all week.* I was wrong. The next morning, when I went into work, something even crazier was waiting for me.

41. Something Crazier (and Smaller) Than a Gun

Mr. Rodolfo was already there. He stood behind the counter, leaning on his arms, a blank expression on his face. *Weird.*

"I thought I was scheduled this morning."

Mr. Rodolfo didn't respond. The drawer of the cash register was open. He was staring into it, apparently zombiefied. Was it my imagination, or was the float in the register fuller than usual?

"Looks like we had a good night."

He slammed the register shut. The counter trembled.

"What's that supposed to mean?"

"Doesn't mean anything," I told him. "I was just saying— cuz the register looks full."

"There's more to life than money. Don't they teach you that in school?"

It was an odd comment, coming from him. It went against his whole good-for-business philosophy of life. I was about to point this out, when I had another surprise. The rear door swung open and the Brothers came lumbering in. What were they doing here? It was too early. They didn't come until the afternoon.

Gonzo (I think) had a bucket and JJ (I also think) had a pair of mops, one in each hand. The mop-strings trailed dingy water down the back stairs. Silent as ever, they went over to Ol' Betty, prying open the broken washer's mouth and dumping in the contents of the bucket. A cascade of pinky-grey water sploshed into the drum. Why were they mopping up the back alley? I'd never seen them doing that before.

I turned to Mr. Rodolfo. "What's going on?"

"Nothing," he said. "You can take the morning off."

"Seriously?"

"I mixed up the schedules. Work tonight instead. I'll pay you double, for the full day, since it was my fault."

Back out on the street, I watched the Brothers through the front window. JJ meticulously rinsed off the bucket and mop, while Gonzo came up to the counter, firing little bullets of Portuguese at Mr. Rodolfo.

I walked around the block, until I was standing under the steps that led up to our kitchen. The pavement by the rear entrance to the laundromat was slick with water. The colour was the same pinky-grey I had just seen dumped into Ol' Betty.

I crouched down and wiped the pavement with a fingertip. All I got was a smoky sludge of water and dirt. Then I saw something. A little white cube, just inside the shadow of the bottom step.

It was a die. A single die, with yin and yang symbols for the pips. When I picked it up, I nearly fainted. Not because of what it was, but because of what was on it. Little flecks of something. Red.

The moment I saw them, I couldn't breathe. The only thing that saved me from passing out was closing my hand, hiding the die, wrenching my fist to keep my blood flowing.

Blood.

I took some deep breaths. I stood up. I shoved my fist in my pocket. I started walking. I just wanted to get as far away from the Sit'N'Spin as I possibly could.

42. Jumping to Conclusions

B-Man always carried A-Man's die. *Always*. Like a talisman, like a religious relic—and A-Man was God. B-Man would never give it up. He certainly wouldn't just drop it in the alley behind a laundromat.

I walked ten blocks up Steinway. I walked past the Super Centre, past the school, until it was just a bunch of office buildings. Then I called Calen.

"Hello?"

"Shit, Cal, something happened. I think something bad happened."

"Kaz? What the hell? *What* happened?"

"I think—okay, I think ..."

"Dude, just breathe."

I tried. I took some long, deep breaths.

"Sounds dirty."

I kept panting anyway.

"Just tell me what happened."

"I think my boss killed somebody."

"*What*?! No way."

"Remember the guy we talked to when we needed beer for Toph's? Not the one who actually bought it, but the other guy, the weird one? In that big bomber jacket? When I went out with Zoey, we saw Mr. Rodolfo come after him with the Arbitrator and then—"

"The what?"

"A big *fucking* crowbar!" My voice came out like a whistle. Like I was twelve. Like my balls hadn't dropped.

"That girl, Zoey? She saw it, too? *With a crowbar?* Dude. You need to call the cops."

"We just watched," I said. I felt sick.

"Wait a sec. When you took her to What the Pho? That was, like, *two nights ago.* You and her watched your boss *off a guy with a crowbar* and you're just telling me now? How come you didn't say anything at the movie?"

"He didn't beat him with it. He just stuck it in his face."

Calen didn't get it (not that I was making sense). "But you just said he murdered a guy. *With a crowbar.*"

"No." I tried again to breathe. "The crowbar thing happened a couple nights ago. He didn't beat him or anything, he just waved it around. But then, just now, I came in to work this morning and I found the die. *Remember?* I rolled a two."

"Dude, wait a second. This is important. Did you or did you not witness a murder?"

I put my hand in my pocket. I wanted to take out the die and look at it again, but I couldn't. "There's blood on it," I said.

"Blood?"

"*Yes!* I know cuz I nearly passed out."

"Wait, that's it?"

"That's what?"

"How do you even know it's the same die?"

"I've seen it a bunch of times. It has these little symbols. I know it's his."

"You found a die with some blood on it—no, *maybe* some blood on it—and you think—"

"Yeah, I do."

"Dude, you gotta be sure." Calen's tone had changed. "The police'll shut that whole place down. If you're wrong, it'll be this huge deal and your boss'll shit himself and you'll *definitely* be fired."

"I know."

"But you really think this happened?"

"I do."

"Then you don't have a choice. You gotta call the police."

"I can't."

"It's simple. 9-1-1, yo."

"I can't."

"Why not?"

It wasn't until Calen actually said it—*you gotta call the police*—that I realized I wasn't going to.

"Because," I said, "I don't have enough yet."

"Enough what?"

"I'm just so close," I whispered.

"Enough what?"

"Money."

"Oh, yeah." Calen's voice changed again. It got softer. "For your mom."

"Maybe you're right," I said. "Maybe I'm jumping to conclusions."

43. The Emerson Centre

After I spoke to Calen, I kept wandering the neighbourhood. I circled back through Montgomery Park, past the big wading pool they have for kids. Crowds of them were there, shouting and splashing each other.

I passed a skinny guy in a straw hat. He was selling a bunch of framed photographs laid out on blankets. I don't know why, but I stopped.

It was all these black-and-white photographs of crumbling buildings. A couple of them I recognized as local landmarks. More than half of the buildings were churches, and in every one, the focus was on missing bricks and boarded-up windows, or the fact that they were taken through wire fences thrown up by demolition crews. On the closest corner of the blanket was a picture of the church connected to the rear of the Emerson Centre. When I saw it, something clicked.

If anybody knew where B-Man was, it was A-Man. I took the west exit from the park and headed in that direction.

The Emerson Centre was a rooming house, partially funded by the church, whose steeple towered behind it. When

I got there, I was greeted by three old men on the saggy porch out front. They each smoked a thin, brown cigarette.

"Who are you?" one of them asked me. "New volunteer?" His voice was nearly as gravelly as something off a Shain Cope album.

"I'm not a volunteer. I'm just looking for somebody."

"Who?"

For a second, I didn't know what to say. Did the *A* in A-Man really stand for something?

"I'm a friend of A-Man's. Is he here?"

The youngest of the three, a guy in a wheelchair whose legs only went as far as his knees, nodded. "He's here."

The one with the gravelly voice yelled into the house. *"A-Man! You got a kid here to see you!"*

Half a minute later, A-Man appeared behind the screen door. All I could see was an impressionistic outline: the thinness of his silhouette, the glossy twinkle of his eyes, the dim halo of his skull cap.

A-Man squinted at me. "I forget something down at the laundromat?"

"I just need to ask you something."

"Okay, c'mon in."

At the back of the house, there was a small room with a bed (more of a cot, really) and a square metal and plastic table. His only decorations were a few framed pictures. Most of them featured the same woman. In some, she had a young boy with her, a kid about Nomi's age.

"You look different," said A-Man. "What changed?"

The question was a surprise, and I didn't know how to answer.

"I met a girl."

A-Man grinned. "So that's why you look like your whole world flipped. That what you wanna ask me about?"

"Actually, no. I came about B-Man. Have you seen him?"

A-Man stuck out his lip. "Not since yesterday."

I felt a cold heaviness in my gut. "What happened yesterday?"

"Nothing."

"But you haven't seen him?"

"No big deal. Not like we're married." A-Man's half-closed eyes made a move for one of the photographs but never made it. They stayed settled on me. "B disappears. It's what he does. He'll be gone for a week, sometimes a whole month, and then—*poof*—he's back. Happens all the time. I'm sure you've noticed: not the most predictable guy."

"Okay," I whispered. "That's cool." Maybe I *was* jumping to conclusions.

"How come you came up here to look for him? He in trouble? He do something stupid? "

"No," I said. "Just haven't seen him in a while, so I wondered where he was."

"Keep wondering."

We were silent for a while. My eyes went back to the photographs.

"That's my wife and son," A-Man told me.

"You're married?"

"I was. In my previous life. Those two there were my pinions."

"Your what?"

A-Man stared at the photograph for a long time. "I'm

talking about the machine," he said at last. "When you're born, all that screaming and blood, that's you getting shook loose. After that, for a long time, you're a lost cog, rattling around. Until you find *your pinion*, that one gear that's been missing you. It's the one place where you finally fit and the machine runs properly for once. Those two, they were my pinions."

"Did something happen to them?"

A-Man almost smiled. "That's the problem with pinion gears. The machine's too big. It's too complicated. Sometimes you find your pinion, but *you don't know* you found your pinion. You see what I mean?"

"I think so."

I was about to suggest B-Man was A-Man's new pinion, but that was stupid. He was a pretty poor substitute for a whole family.

A-Man turned away from the photograph. "Guess I'm back to rattling around."

It was odd how there were no pictures with all three of them together. Just ones of the woman and the boy. It made me happy to know I still had the photograph of Dad and me, on the courts at DeWinter Hills.

"So B-Man wanders off sometimes?" I asked.

"*All* the time."

I nodded.

"He wasn't always like that."

A-Man pulled back the door to his bathroom, revealing a framed photograph of a group of men standing together on a brown, rocky slope. They all had guns: large, automatic assault rifles. A-Man was standing at the edge of the group. His goatee was the same, but everything else belonged to a different person. His body was broader, thick arms bursting out of a tight green T-shirt.

"That's B there beside me."

I never would have known. B-Man's face was round and healthy. All his teeth were there, polished white. He showed them off with the beaming grin of an actor.

"No way ..." But once you looked, it was obvious.

"Like I said, a previous life." A-Man stood beside me, arms folded and gripping his sides. "You make one bad decision, or in B's case, one *good* decision, and the whole machine'll flip."

"What decision?"

A-Man squinted at me. "I never tell you?"

I shook my head.

"B took a bullet for me. Right here." He tapped his head, just behind his ear. "Only grazed him, but he was out cold for three months. When he came to, he wasn't the same person, and neither was I."

B-Man never pulled down the hood of his bomber jacket, even in summer. I had always assumed it was part of his craziness, and maybe it was. Or maybe it was his way of disguising the wound.

"He saved your life."

A-Man nodded. "After that, I lost the stomach for it. He was my best friend till then, and now he's ..."

"He still is," I said, cutting in. "He's B-Man."

A-Man didn't say anything.

I wanted to tell him I had found the die in the alley, but I didn't want him to worry. I wanted to believe B-Man was just wandering around somewhere, disappearing for a few days like he always did. That was true, but there was another reason

I left the die in my pocket, a reason I couldn't quite admit to myself: I wanted to keep my job going, just a bit longer. I was so close.

"You're right," I said, as if A-Man needed reassuring. "He'll be back soon."

Walking back from the Centre, I felt numb. What snapped me out of it was my phone, vibrating against my leg. The display said it was the library where Mom worked, but when I picked up, it wasn't her.

"Is this ..." There was a pause while whoever it was tried to make sense of my name. "*Ka...zoo...oh* Barrett?"

"Kaz," I said.

"Your mother is Aiko Barrett?"

"Yes."

"I'm afraid your mother's had some sort of an ... episode."

44. Hairy-Terry

In the hospital bed, Mom's face was pale and damp. Her hair clung to her forehead in sinister curls, like she was floating through weeds in a lake.

"Is she okay?" Nomi asked.

"She's just sleeping."

"She looks hot. She's sweating."

I brushed back Mom's hair, smoothing it away from her face.

"Do you think we'll get it, too?"

"Get what?"

"The disease."

"It's super rare. You don't need to worry."

"But she's our mom. Katie told me she had an uncle who got cancer from his father, who got cancer from *his* father. She said it's hairy-terry."

"*Hereditary.* Somnitis isn't like that. It's not contagious, either."

"How do you know?"

"I've read a lot about it. Nobody knows why it happens."

Nomi covered her eyes. She never liked watching Mom asleep.

"You shouldn't worry about that stuff," I told her.

"Can I stay at Jenn's?"

"What? Tonight?"

Nomi nodded. "Until Mom gets home."

"It could be a couple days. I don't know if—wait, who's Jenn?"

"*Jennifer!* I told you, she plays violin! And they have an upright."

"A what?"

"An upright piano!"

It stung a little that my kid sister didn't want to hang out with her big bro, but only a little. If Nomi wanted to have a slumber party with Jennifer and an upright piano, it'd mean I'd have the house to myself.

"Okay, well, if Jenn's parents are fine with you staying over, then ..."

"I already called them from home. They said it was fine."

"Great," I said. "So we're all set."

45. Simple

While Nomi packed for the sleepover, I skulked off to my room and called Zoey. She didn't pick up, so I left a message saying I hoped we could hang out soon and, in case she wasn't doing anything that night, it looked like my mom would be away, so maybe after I finished work, around ten or so, maybe we could ... et cetera. It was one of those rambling messages you regret halfway through, at which point it's too late to turn back, so you just keep going.

When Jennifer and her mom came to pick up Nomi, I noticed how strikingly this other mother differed from ours. She was a plump woman, with stylish, thick-rimmed glasses and brightly coloured clothes.

"Oh, Jennifer's so excited!" she kept saying. "She's been talking about this all day!"

Jennifer, meanwhile, sat in the back of the minivan, waving at my sister with all the enthusiasm of Becky Leighton.

As soon as they were gone, I went into the Sit'N'Spin. I didn't see Mr. Rodolfo, meaning he was either out back or in the basement. Sliding by the counter, my jeans rubbed the wood and I felt something dig into my thigh. It was the die.

Even though I'd changed into a fresh pair of jeans, I couldn't help transferring it into the new pocket. Like B-Man, it had become my talisman.

Mr. Rodolfo must have heard me come in because he creaked up from the basement.

"I'm taking off. You close up, okay?"

I nodded and watched him go. After that, I kept checking my phone, looking for a call from Zoey, but there was nothing. I made some change for a young couple who came in, wanting to put a drenched canvas tent in one of the dryers. I let them, even though I was pretty sure Mr. Rodolfo would have said no.

Later, I went out back and crouched in the alley. The ground was dry. I couldn't see anything that looked like blood. I opened Ol' Betty's mouth and peered down her throat. She was wiped so clean she sparkled. I went back to the counter and stood at the top of the stairs, swaying on the threshold of the basement.

The Arbitrator hung on the wall as always. It was black and shiny, as if it had been recently polished. Then again, I had never examined it closely before; maybe it always shined like that. Either way, there certainly wasn't any blood on it, at least none I could see.

I stood on the stairs for a long time. I remembered what Mr. Rodolfo had told me when I first started working there. *Down there's my space, understand? Upstairs—your space. Downstairs— my space. Simple, yeah?*

Simple.

I tiptoed down the steps.

At the bottom was an open area, a medium-sized room with the walls exposed, showing off struts and wiring. Under the stairs was the door to Mr. Rodolfo's office, while on the far side was the door to the poker room. I tried that one first.

To my surprise, it wasn't locked. The walls of the room were pasted over with fake wooden pressboard. In the middle of the room was a large round table with metal legs, surrounded by chairs. The tabletop was marred by the sticky, overlapping circles left by coffee mugs and beer glasses. The only other piece of furniture was a low white bookshelf, featuring a plastic tray of poker chips, some weathered notepads and two DIY books about washing machines and bathroom tiling. That was it. Mr. Rodolfo's poker fortress was basically just a room with some chairs and a table. If there was anything to find down here, I thought, it would be in his office.

Which (of course) was locked.

46. I ♥ NY

After my shift, I went out into the street. A wet, gloomy warmth rose off the pavement. It was that mysterious time on a summer night when you can walk from inside to outside without any perceptible change in temperature. There's something eerie about that. Eerie, but intriguing. Maybe that was why I didn't go upstairs right away. Instead, I wandered across the street and stood in the place where Zoey played.

The tiny clipping from the *Chronicler* was still taped up in Dave Mizra's window. Now that I knew he had made up that story, it looked smaller, shabbier, the tape fading to a sickly yellow. It was becoming clear that although Dave Mizra dressed like a hipster, listened to cool music and had pretensions of being an artist, his store was basically a pawnshop.

I put my forehead against the glass. Inside was a trio of glassed-in counters arranged in a U-shape. It looked like a conventional jewellers. The only difference was the large, framed, black-and-white photograph on the back wall. Why had I never noticed that before?

It was a framed poster of a thickly bearded man with wild hair and narrow eyes. He was wearing an *I ♥ NY* T-shirt, standing in an alley with one arm raised above his head, fingers hooked into the grill of a fire escape. From the dim glow of the street lamps out front, he almost looked real, like he might step off the wall, smoke spiralling from his cigarette.

It was Shain Cope. That same image was in the French liner notes of *Freudian Slap*.

"Planning a robbery?"

Startled, I pulled away from the window.

It was Zoey. Even with the rattler slung across her back, she had somehow snuck up on me. I must have been really out of it. She was back to her goth-slash-punk look: black skirt, black shirt, black leggings, with the silver and leather jewellery that seemed to be an extension of her instrument.

"How long have you been standing there?"

"About a second."

My forehead left a foggy oval of grease on the glass. I tried wiping it away but it only smeared. "What did you just ask me?"

She laughed. "I asked if you were planning a robbery. You looked pretty suspicious, staring in the window of a closed jewellery shop."

"I was just looking."

"That's cool. I got your message. Am I too late to hang out?"

"No, I think my mom's gonna be gone … all night, probably."

"So what do you wanna do?" she asked, glancing across the street at the Sit'N'Spin. "Were you just gonna hang out around your work?"

"I was hanging around because—well, that's where I live." I pointed to the windows above the laundromat. Most of the time, our apartment embarrassed me, but after seeing where Zoey lived, it didn't seem so bad.

"A while back, my dad and I lived in an apartment like that, above a row of shops. That was in Prague."

"Where?"

"Czechoslovakia. Over there, it's called a *konírny*. It means 'mews,' a row of apartments that once had stables under them." She pronounced it *ko-neer-nay*, with a curl to her tongue that sounded authentic.

"Is that where you're from? Czechoslovakia?"

"We just lived there for a while, but yeah, in a *konírny*."

"Because of your dad's work?"

She nodded sadly. "I've lived all over. Europe, Mexico City, Montreal, New York, California—*LA was crazy!* I hated it. You couldn't walk anywhere." She shook her head, recalling something amusing, but something she didn't care to share. "Sorry I freaked out the other night. I don't think it's cool my dad keeps a gun in the house, but I kind of understand. He just wants to protect us."

"*I'm* the one who freaked out. I thought you wanted to give it to me."

"What, like a present?"

"You said you 'had something for me,' and then when I opened the drawer …"

"Well, yeah, but not *a gun!*"

"This is gonna sound weird, but for a second, I thought you wanted me to kill somebody."

She threw her head back and laughed. It came out in a juddering machine gun of *HA-HA-HA*s. "You're crazy!"

She was laughing so hard, it got me started, too, but then it hit me that we were cackling away about killing somebody.

A picture of B-Man flashed in my head. I couldn't keep the laughter going.

Zoey stopped, too. "My dad pulls stupid shit sometimes." She looked across the street again, at the two front windows of our apartment. "It's all dark."

I nodded. "My sister's sleeping over at a friend's."

"Then I guess it's your turn to give *me* a tour."

47. You Always Remember Your Second Time

So I finally got it right. What surprised me most were the things that stuck in my head: The way Zoey's instrument made the softest noise in the world when she propped it against the wall in the entranceway. How, for no good reason, my tour of the apartment ended in the laundry room, which was where we started to kiss. How we made out going up the hall and finally into my bedroom, and how exciting it was to leave the door open—just a crack—because no one else was there. How, when Zoey was naked, her body was so white she looked frosted in ice, and how the illusion was foiled by a bruise on the outside of her leg, just smaller than a fist. How natural it felt to finally know what I was doing. How it wasn't until afterwards, when she rolled onto her stomach, that I noticed her tattoo: a rectangular criss-cross of black lines, spreading across the small of her back.

It was a single bar of music.

"What is it?" I asked her, running my fingers over the notes.

"You don't recognize it?"

I tried to hear the song in my head, but I had never been very good at reading music.

"I played it for you. On piano."

"*Clair de Lune?*"

She nodded.

"Is it your favourite song?"

"Maybe. It's so, *so* beautiful."

"Then how come you never play it? On your instrument, I mean."

"I do, but only sometimes."

She rolled over and put her head on my chest. Her dreads were smoother than they looked, but they still tickled. I picked up a strand as thick as my thumb, twirling it against the skin of her arm.

"Can I ask you something?"

"Depends," she said.

"On what?"

"*Duh*. On what the question is."

"You ever think about love at first sight?"

She laughed. "You mean like seeing me walk past a laundromat and thinking, 'check it out, it's the new messiah'? Because trust me, you've *definitely* got the wrong person."

"Okay, but that wasn't really the first time I saw you."

"I thought it was."

"It was and it wasn't. When you walked past, I noticed you, but I didn't *see* you. What I saw most was the instrument. And your clothes, your hair, but not you. Not your face. That wasn't until we were out back at Toph's, under the gazebo."

"So you're saying you believe in it?" She sounded surprised.

"I don't know. I'm just asking."

"I'm sure it happens sometimes," she said in that older voice of hers, the one that seemed to come and go at random.

"Is this what you want to do? Like, forever?"

"It's nice, isn't it?"

"Not *this*-this," I said. Then I reconsidered. "I mean, sure, screwing forever would be—well, yeah, nice—but I'm fairly sure there would be unforeseen ramifications."

"Chafing, for instance."

I laughed. "I meant the question in a more general sense. I mean moving from school to school, playing music on the street. Don't you ever want to play somewhere else? Like somewhere, I dunno … *better?*" I regretted how much it sounded like an insult.

Zoey didn't seem to mind. "As long as I get to play, I don't care about anything else. I don't care what the music is, I don't even care about the *instrument*. I'll make one myself if I have to, like I did with the rattler. That's the deal, get it?"

"What deal?"

"The one I have with my dad." Her voice turned harder than I'd ever heard it. "He drags me around, but no matter where we go, I always get to play my music. It's the only thing that keeps me going."

We were silent again. It didn't feel right to keep toying with Zoey's hair. I let the one thick dread drop on the pillow.

"Okay, maybe you're right. If I had my choice, I'd go to Europe. To London or Paris or Rome. They have some crazy music schools over there. Classic, *ancient* places. I'd go there and study."

"You should," I said, but I realized I didn't mean it. I didn't want her to go anywhere. I stared at my jeans, lying in a puddle of denim on the floor. "Maybe for now, your dad could get you into classes at Falconer. They must have a decent program."

"*Into where?* Oh, yeah, Falconer." She picked up the same dread I had plopped on the pillow, examining the tip. "That place is a hole."

Suddenly, Zoey seemed bored. I wanted to say something to impress her.

"I think my boss killed somebody."

"*What?*" She lifted her head off my chest and sat up, folding herself in my blankets. "Say that again."

I told her everything. About A-Man and B-Man, about finding the die, the Brothers, the pinky-grey water they poured into Ol' Betty, how Mr. Rodolfo had unexpectedly taken over my shift.

"I knew it," she said when I was finished. "I *told* you he was a mobster."

"What do you think I should do? You think I should tell someone?"

"You just told me."

"I mean the police."

She narrowed her eyes. "They'll want some proof."

I got out of bed, dipped one hand in the pocket of my jeans and took out the die.

"*That's* your proof?"

"I think that's blood on it."

"Where? It's just a die with goofy-looking spots."

"But what about—" I forced myself to concentrate on the little chunk of plastic, but what I saw didn't make me queasy. It didn't make the room cloud over in grey. It didn't make me faint.

"Shit. It must have rubbed off in my pocket." I held the die up for a closer look, but there was nothing there.

"Did you actually see this happen?"

"No."

Zoey winced at me, the way you screw up your face in sympathy when you see someone get kicked in the balls. "I can tell you, the police are gonna want more than just that." She meant the die, which looked puny and pathetic in my hand. "If you do wanna call them, I'd suggest putting on some clothes first."

I realized I was standing in the middle of the room in nothing but a floppy condom. My whole body blushed.

Zoey giggled. "I was just gonna say—not the best look for you."

I jammed B-Man's die back into the pocket of my disembodied jeans and dove into bed. Once I had wormed into my underwear, we tangled our bodies together again. Dearborn once told us that we'd be able to tell we had got it right when, afterwards, we just wanted to lie there with the other person, just staring at each other. Turns out he was right.

"So if you aren't sure," Zoey said after a while, "what are you gonna do?"

"No matter what happens—if I'm wrong or if I'm right—I'll still lose my job. And I need it. I'm so close to having enough."

Zoey's brow knotted together in the middle. "Saving for school's that important? As long as you get your ten grand saved for college, who cares about anything else?"

"*Twelve*. I need to save twelve thousand. I'm almost there."

She sighed heavily and her body shrunk away. "Money," she said, and that was all.

"I know, it can really screw stuff up. It's the same with Dave Mizra."

"Huh?" She rolled back to me, this deeply curious look on her face. The shift to Dave Mizra was a leap she couldn't quite grasp. "What do you mean?"

"I mean money screwed up everything for him, too. Poor guy. I really feel sorry for him."

"Why? What happened to him?"

"He's broke," I told her. "He might have to sell his shop."

Zoey sat up. "Really? Where'd you hear that?"

"He told me himself. Besides, this is Evandale. Even the rich people are broke. It's kind of a prerequisite for living here."

"But I thought—I mean, doesn't he brag to people about how much cash he makes, like with his custom jewellery or whatever? I thought Veronica Heller shopped there."

"He made that up. It was a lie he told the *Chronicler* because he thought it would drum up business. Only it didn't. Kind of a dumb thing to do, if you ask me. I'm sure he could get in trouble for lying like that."

"Shit." Zoey thumped backward on the bed, her dreads drumming the pillow.

"What's the problem?"

"I guess I feel sorry for the guy, too."

"You do?"

"Also, I think I should go."

"You don't have to. My sister's gone until at least tomorrow afternoon, and my mom—I don't think she'll be home till then either."

"I can't."

"Wait, what's the rush?"

"I just remembered. My dad'll be home tonight. He'll kill me if I'm not there."

"It's not that late."

"Sorry." She rolled her head back and forth, searching the bed. "Where's my bra?"

"On the floor."

"Don't be mad. I just really have to go, that's all."

"We can do this again, though, right? Like, next time we get a chance?"

She sat up, tucking one pink dreadlock behind her ear, her eyes sparkling. "Next time we get a chance."

48. My Piece of the Puzzle

Late the following afternoon, both Mom and Nomi were back at home. Mom zoned out in front of the TV and Nomi curled up beside her. It was hard to believe Zoey had been here the night before. I could still feel the leanness of her body, her warm skin pressed against my back.

I thought about what A-Man told me in his room at the Emerson Centre, about pinions and loose gears, all spinning around in an endless machine. After everything that had happened—Dad dying; us moving to this crappy corner of Evandale; Mom getting sick; Mr. Rodolfo giving me a job—after all that, you had to wonder if I was *meant* to be here. If any of those things hadn't happened, I would never have met Zoey. Maybe the two of us were cogs that fit. That was certainly how it felt.

It was nice to think about, but unfortunately, the idea kept getting crowded out by thoughts of B-Man.

Proof. Zoey said I needed proof. She seemed to know what she was talking about. If I was brave enough, I could snoop around the laundromat. When I came out of my room, Mom was there in the hall.

"You okay?"

"I'm fine." She pointed to the bathroom. "I've been drinking a lot of water."

"Are we going to Beauhaven?"

"I'm not really feeling up to it quite yet."

She wasn't kidding. She looked even worse than after the last attack.

"It's okay," she said, with a weak smile. "In a few days, we'll drive up. I'll get some treatment, and who knows? This could be the last one I have for a while. Maybe the last one, period."

"Maybe." It occurred to me that this was the first attack she had had at the library. "Are you going back to work?"

"Of course." She said it a little too quickly to be believed. "First, I'll need a little time off."

"How much?"

She took a step into the bathroom. "Why don't you go spend some time with Nomi. I'm not sure if you've noticed, but she might be the one who needs some attention. Not me."

Nomi was in the living room, sucked in by the latest episode of *Big Daddy*.

"Didn't I tell you not to watch that?"

She ignored me.

"Hey, I just thought of something. Maybe I could teach you some stuff. We could get out the old Casio."

Nomi was so shocked to hear this, she actually deigned to mute the television. Then she turned to me with this weirdly mature, weirdly apologetic face. "That's nice," she said, "but you don't have to."

"What?"

"I changed my mind."

"You did? When?"

"Remember Jennifer?"

"Um, yeah." I couldn't see what this had to do with Nomi changing her mind about the piano.

"Well, guess what?" she said.

"What?"

"Jenny says she's gonna teach me *the violin!*"

49. Snooping Around the Sit'N'Spin, Part 1

Mr. Rodolfo didn't say a word to me when I went down to work. That was fine by me. To be honest, I wasn't sure what to say to him. If I could avoid him, I thought, I could also avoid all the speculations in my head about mobsters and money and murder.

After he left, I started a methodical search of the entire laundromat. I pretended to clean everything, but in reality, I was examining it. One by one, I poked my head into every washer and dryer in the place. Finally, I took a paper towel, closed my eyes and wiped around Ol' Betty's innards.

"Hey!" someone yelled at me. "You lose something down there?"

I flinched so hard my knees gave out and I bashed them on the washer. Up near the windows, a fat guy in a wife-beater was sitting on the benches, waiting for a load to finish.

"No," I said to him. "Just cleaning!" To prove it, I held up the perfectly pristine, perfectly dry paper towel in my hand. *Dry and pristine.* (If Ol' Betty had been force-fed B-Man's blood, she hadn't got any of it stuck in her teeth.)

"Just cleaning, huh?" asked the fat guy.

"Yep."

"You're pretty thorough."

It sounded like he was making fun of me, so I didn't answer him. I took a peek into the back alley. The wooden stairs that led up to our kitchen looked the same as ever. The pavement that had been moist with the Brothers' mop water was bone dry.

My phone buzzed. I hoped it was Zoey. Maybe her dad was away, maybe she wanted to hook up again, but no, it was only a text from Calen. The subject line said: AWESOME NEWS!!

50. Calen's Welcome (but Not Quite as Sexy) News

Calen: DUDE!! guess who got 3 tics to WBB @ Foo Bar 2nite?

Me: WBB??

Calen: WILD BLUE BOUNCE! U, me, Alana.

Me: Uh ... how much for tickets?

Calen: FREE! My bro cant go, so I got em.

Me: can we get 4?

Calen: 3's all I got. totly sold out.

Me: k, cool

Calen: what's the earliest I can pick u up?

51. Snooping Around the Sit'N'Spin, Part 2

Just before closing, the Sit'N'Spin was nearly empty. Once it was just me and a bored-looking DIYer waiting for his dryer to stop tumbling, I crept downstairs. This time, I moved slowly, carefully searching every inch of the place. All I found were some old crates, some old shelves, boxes of supplies and tools, decrepit brooms and mops and the big pressboard poker table surrounded by its crappy metal chairs. There was nothing incriminating at all, nothing to imply Mr. Rodolfo and his Brothers had recently murdered a homeless man.

At that point, I was ready to give up. I would try to forget about B-Man (something I already did most of the time). There was no real proof something had happened to him, and A-Man knew his friend better than anyone. If he said B-Man was off on one of his jaunts, he probably was. If it got to be the end of summer and he still hadn't shown up, then I could tell someone about what I'd seen. By that time, I would have saved enough money and it wouldn't matter. That's what I told myself, at least.

I was just about to climb back up the stairs, when my hand, almost with a mind of its own, reached out for the doorknob to Mr. Rodolfo's office. I expected to hear the same sound I heard last time, the stubborn *chk-chk* of the lock, but instead the doorknob turned. His office was open.

I had never seen the inside, not even when Mr. Rodolfo had interviewed me for the job; he had asked his questions over the counter upstairs.

I found a light switch, and a pair of fluorescent tubes buzzed to life. The office wasn't much bigger than my bedroom. There was a dark-green metal desk, a coffee table and a couple plastic chairs stacked against the cement wall. The surface of the desk was scattered with papers and several tin cans that bristled with pens. Against one wall was a beige bookcase. Nearly every shelf was piled with wires, outdated stereo equipment and crappy speakers. The top shelf was home to a handful of mystery novels and men's magazines, ones with articles on how to get the most out of a sit-up. In the corner was a metal filing cabinet with an old TV perched on top. On the floor beside the cabinet was a set of barbells. They were unused, all four of them hairy with dust.

I searched the various shelves and drawers but I didn't find anything. Just the usual stuff—papers, files, office supplies. In the bottom of the filing cabinet, I found several boxes of playing cards and a case of poker chips.

Between the cabinet and the desk was another door. When I tried to open it, it was locked; it gave off the *chk-chk* noise I had expected to hear a moment ago. I put my ear to the wood. I didn't hear anything. Very gently, I knocked. There was no answer, but then—

"*Hello? Anybody here?*" someone shouted.

I nearly shit myself. But then I realized the voice hadn't come from the other side of the door. It had come from upstairs.

52. Gigabot Productions

The guy at the counter was tall, middle-aged and handsome in a daytime soap opera kind of way. On his face, he wore a thick, brown goatee and glasses with rims to match (thick and brown). The sleeves of his shiny grey suit were rolled up, showing off forearms roped with muscle. He was using his fingers to drum a beat on the edge of the counter, upon which was lumped a pile of clothes. All suits.

"Can I help you?"

His bright blue eyes flashed toward the entrance. "Says there you're still open. Are you?"

"We close at ten."

"You do dry cleaning, yeah?"

"What do you need?"

He separated the pile on the counter. "These are all suits, tops and bottoms. I need them dry cleaned and pressed." His voice was light and smooth and calm, but confident. You could tell he was used to getting what he wanted. "No huge rush, but I need them by Thursday morning. Got it?"

I told him it wouldn't be a problem.

"Great, we're shooting all day Friday and then over the weekend."

"Shooting?"

"Just a pilot."

"*Pilot?* Like a TV show?"

He wrinkled his nose like somebody farted. "We haven't been picked up yet, but it seems like we got legs. The thing could really run."

"Cool." No wonder he was so confident, so out of place next to the usual people who came into the Sit'N'Spin. "So are you, like, an actor?"

He chuckled and shook his head. "Producer. I'm the guy who signs the cheques. And occasionally drops off the dry cleaning, apparently." He sighed and patted the heap of suits.

I asked him if he was shooting around here, in Evandale. He explained that his crew had rented one of the old houses down at the bottom of Emerson and they were using it as the set.

"This neighbourhood has a nice feel to it. Urban, gritty, right? Everybody's looking for that, so it's good when you find it. My second unit DOP says the light's good, too, 'specially round sunset." He smiled. "I wouldn't know."

I smiled back, mostly because his grin was contagious, not because I understood what he was talking about. "Second unit DOP" meant nothing to me.

"It's a great neighbourhood," he went on, gazing out the window. "*And cheap*. If we get picked up, we'll definitely shoot a few episodes around here."

I felt a little stab of jealousy. How nice would it be if the only reason you came to Evandale was to make a TV show?

"The next couple of days, it's just pickups and cutaways. All second unit stuff, but I like to be here to get the details right. Sets the mood. Principle photography won't start for another week, but there's still a shitload to do. Pardon my French."

"Who's in it?" I asked. "Anybody famous?"

"Sorry, kid, that's classified. But stick around. I might let something slip." He smiled again, this time with a mischievous glint.

I liked the way his eyes were so bright and self-assured. I liked the way he called me "kid," like I was his sidekick.

"Wait," I said, just as he turned to leave. Then I realized I didn't have anything to say. "Uh ... you want us to call you if we get the suits done early?"

"Doubt I'll have time to come get 'em. Too busy with prep."

"Oh, sure," I said, like I knew everything in the world about preparing to shoot a pilot.

"But you never know." He reached into his pocket and took out a silver card case. "You can get me here."

His business card featured a blocky, crayon doodle of a robot—square head, metallic pincers, light bulbs for ears. It said:

Andrew Myers
Gigabot Productions

After that, he jogged across the street to where he had parked, right in front of Mizra's Fire & Ice. His car was a glittering red convertible. In a neighbourhood like Evandale, a ride like that was even more conspicuous than one of Dave Mizra's suits.

53. First Times

Calen used his brother's ID and I had a licence from one of his brother's friends, a Sikh kid named Vijay Sandu (who really did look like me). Calen was explicit about keeping the ID safe.

"Lose this," Calen explained, passing me the little rectangle of plastic, "and Veej says he'll gut you—like, literally. He's not even kidding. He doesn't tell anyone, but he carries a ceremonial dagger."

"Part of his religion," Alana added.

Foo Bar is an old nightclub in midtown. It opened in the seventies and was made famous by all the singers and bands adored by Dave Mizra, people like Shain Cope.

"You see that homeless girl again?" Calen asked me.

"Stop saying that. She's *not* homeless."

Calen mocked me with a sulk.

"But, yeah, I did. She stayed over last night."

Alana was surprised. "*Really?* That was fast."

Calen wanted details, but I wasn't prepared to give any, especially not in the cheek-to-cheek, factory-farm lineup outside Foo Bar. Or ever. It was something I wanted to keep for myself. It was dawning on me that it was possible to have *two* first times. First, there was the actual, official (and almost certainly disastrous) first time, and then there was something much better. The first time you actually knew what you were doing. I had a very strong suspicion that years later, it was Zoey I would remember, not Becky Leighton.

The air inside Foo Bar was clammy with sour beer reek and evaporating sweat. A local band, two guys and a girl with acoustic guitars and a tambourine, played on the stage. Some of Alana's friends were already there, clustered around a table near the front. Alana joined them, while Calen and I went to get beers.

"So last night," he said, while we waited at the bar. "You gonna tell me what happened?"

"It was a good night. That's all I'm saying."

"Dude! *Awesome.*"

"It kinda was."

Calen shuffled his feet, something he didn't do often. "I know I made fun of you, but hey, I gotta admit, she's a pretty cool girl. Pretty hot, too."

"*I know!*" (I might have said it with a bit too much relish.) "I wish she could've come tonight."

We scored our beers and raised a toast to other people's driver's licences. On the way back to the table, someone tapped me on the shoulder. *Zoey*, I thought. But when I turned around, it wasn't her. It was Topher Briggs.

"*Kaz!*" He yelled at me over the music. "How're you doin'?!"

I was ready to defend myself from a fist to the face, but instead he put one hand on my shoulder. "Listen, sorry about what happened at my place. I was *suuuper* kacked. Obviously."

"You still are, looks like."

"Yep!" He raised his own pint glass. "But seriously. I'm sorry, okay?"

"Seriously?"

He nodded. "You're gonna hafta show me around sometime."

"What?"

"Didn't you hear? The whole family's moving to the neighbourhood!"

"Evandale?" I thought he was making fun of me. "Shut up."

"I'm serious! You know my folks, yeah? Their bank took a huge hit. My dad got the axe, and next month, we heard they're cutting my mom's whole division."

"Shit," said Calen. "Is that true?"

"It's another 'global economic crisis.' Fucking new one every week." Topher turned to me. "Don't be surprised when we move in down the block, okay?" He clinked his glass against mine, spilling a dollop of foam on the floor. "Here's to the new neighbourhood!"

Topher looked dejected. I wanted to say something to cheer him up. "It's not so bad, actually. They're shooting a movie down there. Like, right around the corner from me."

His face brightened. "Really? What movie?"

"Actually, it's just a pilot for TV. But they're gonna shoot the whole series there."

Calen and Topher nodded like they knew what I was talking about. I thought I might have to answer more questions, but Calen turned to Topher instead.

"I'm sure your folks'll figure something out."

"Maybe," Toph said, but he didn't sound convinced.

"Anyway, I'm sorry I hit you in front of your girl—who is *crazy*, by the way." He came closer and threw an arm over my shoulders. "Also, I'm sorry we didn't stay friends after, y'know, your dad died."

"Whatever. Don't worry about it."

"C'mon," he said, pulling me toward the back of the bar. "A bunch of us have a table upstairs."

I looked to Calen, but he said he had to bring Alana her drink; he would come find us later. Upstairs, there was a whole other floor. It was darker, full of shadows, the sort of place from which Zoey might emerge, shimmering like a mirage. (She didn't.)

Becky was at a table on the edge of the balcony, overlooking the stage. ("*Oh-mi-god*, Kaz!" Cue customary wave.) Topher slid in beside her and gave her a sloppy, off-target kiss. Then there was a bunch of people I didn't know. The only other one of the crowd I recognized was Christina Muñoz, perched daintily on the end of the curving bench. She was in this pale green, skin-tight dress, more suited to a dance club, not a hipster dive like Foo Bar. She looked uncomfortable, which was a first.

"It's you," she said to me, which was unexpected.

"Me?"

"Kaz, right?"

"Yeah," I said. Another first: Christina Muñoz knew my name.

"I heard Topher say it when he saw you, over the balcony."

"Oh. Right."

"But, yeah, I remember you from Toph's party. Hard to forget when they drag you away with blood all over." She screwed up her face. "*Gross.*"

I pointed at Toph. "Blame him."

"Is he gonna punch you again, because I don't want blood on my dress."

I laughed because I thought it was a joke, but then I realized Christina was serious. "No, it's okay. I think we just made up."

"Cool."

She slid sideways to let me in. I noticed (how could I not?) the dress inching up her legs. I joined her on the bench and I could feel the other guys at the table watching us.

She examined my face. "We were at the same school when we were kids, right?"

"Only for a couple years. I moved away in eighth grade. Rosemount Middle School. You remember that?"

She nodded. "Sort of. You're kind of Chinese, right?"

"Kind of Japanese. I'm half. My dad's from Barbados. *Was* from Barbados. He died."

"Yeah, my next-door neighbour died when I was ten. And I'm kind of mixed up, too, by the way. My mom's from Bogotá, in Colombia. And my dad's from Peru. Guess we kind of have a lot in common."

I wasn't sure Colombian-slash-Peruvian was quite the same thing, seeing as the two countries were beside each other and the people there both spoke Spanish. I also wasn't convinced a dead neighbour was the same as a dead dad. But I didn't mention any of this. Having a regular conversation with Christina Muñoz was too much of a novelty.

"Have you ever noticed," she asked me, looking at the backs of her hands, "it's always the mixed-up people who're the best looking?"

"Huh?"

"My mom used to breed show dogs, like when I was a kid,

but she stopped because they kept dying of all these weird diseases. Basically, cuz they're inbred, right? Then, after she quit the business, you know what kind of dog she bought?"

Where was this going?

"I have no idea," I said.

"A mongrel! A total *mutt*! Get it?"

"Not really."

"My mom was like, if you want good genes, you gotta mix them up. I think it's the same with people. Like you and me."

"Wait, you really think that?"

She shrugged. "Only cuz it's true."

"But, um …" I started squirming, actually fidgeting on the end of the bench. "You don't think that sounds kinda, I dunno … kinda racist?"

"What? *No!* Racist is, like, crazy guys in hoods! It's, like, *burning* people, and that other thing. Whaddaya call it? Starts with an *L*. Hanging people from trees."

"Lynching?"

"Yeah! Lynching. *That's* racist." She waved her hand between her and me. "This is just a fact. Mixed-up people are the hottest." She shrugged like this was a perfectly normal thing to say. Then she switched gears again. "Do you smoke?"

"No."

She pushed me off the end of the bench and got out, pulling down the hem of her skirt.

"Come on. Even if you don't, you can't let me go have a ciggie by myself."

She led me toward the stairs, unsteady on her high heels. On the middle landing, there was a painted black door to the back "patio," an empty sandlot with a fence around it, lit by the glow of a 7-Eleven on the far side. The bouncer guarding the exit was massive; hollow out one of his legs, and you could plop me right inside.

"You should stand up straighter," Christina said, once we were alone.

"Thanks for the tip."

She lit a cigarette and took me by the shoulders. Smoke coiled around my ear as she pushed and pulled me until my back was straight. "You're pretty decent looking, at least when you're not slouching."

"Yeah, thanks," I said, with only a tinge of sarcasm. Meanwhile, I could feel my spine trying to straighten itself.

"You heard about me and Devon, right?"

"No."

"We broke up."

"Really? When?"

She rolled her eyes. "Like, the same week we got together, he was already cheating on me with some girl from his school. Total slut!" She took a deep drag on her cigarette. "You got a girlfriend?"

I wasn't sure how to answer, so I said, "Yeah, I guess so."

"You *guess* so? I hope she doesn't hear you talk about her like that."

"It's cuz we just met, like a couple weeks ago."

"Cool. How'd you meet her?"

"At Toph's party."

"Wait. The girl who played piano?"

"She's pretty good, huh?"

"Yeah, except that she's *crazy!* You should've seen her after Topher knocked you out. I thought she was going to kill him! *She's* your girlfriend? Seriously?"

"We just started, but yeah."

Her head fell sideways and she looked at me closely again. "Guess I missed my chance."

It was weird hearing Christina—*the* Christina Muñoz— say that. "Maybe I should have stood up straighter," I said, laughing a little. "You might've noticed me."

"Maybe," she said, coming closer. "You have a nice mouth, anyway. Devon's got a mouth like yours. People with sort of puffy lips like you—and me—that's how you can tell a good kisser." I wondered if Christina always looked for bits of herself in other people. I was still wondering when she leaned forward and kissed me.

I was so stunned I just stood there. I may have even kissed her back. A little.

Then there was this loud *BANG*. It was the door beside us flinging open. I pushed Christina away in time to see the giant bouncer throwing someone out the door—like, actually throwing. *Through the air.*

It was Zoey.

54. F.U.B.A.R.

"You're banned," said the bouncer. "Don't come back. I remember faces."

Zoey lay on the gravel in a pile of crinoline, leather and dreads. She looked like a goth pixie—a dead one.

"I hope you know you just broke my *fucking* arm!" she screamed.

The bouncer didn't give a shit. "I'll believe you when you sue us."

"Maybe I will."

"Go ahead. See what happens. We'll tell 'em the shit you just pulled in here. Now *fuck off.*"

I stepped between them. "You can't talk to her like that."

"Who're you?"

"Her boyfriend."

He looked past me at Christina. "Then I'd say you've got some explaining to do."

Zoey sat up, her arm folded against her side, her eyes glossy with tears. *"Look what you did!"* She raised her elbow to show off the back of her arm, where a mottled yellow bruise spread all the way up to her shoulder. *"See?!"*

The bouncer laughed. "I didn't do that."

"Who did then?!"

"How should I know? Maybe your 'boyfriend' here. Either way, now's the time to—*Fuck. Off.* Okay?"

He vanished inside, slamming the door.

Christina swayed on her feet. "Did he lock it just now?" she asked no one in particular. "Can we get back in, or do we hafta go around?"

I pretended Christina wasn't there.

"Should I call an ambulance?" I asked Zoey.

"No," she said quietly, "I was lying. My arm's not broken."

Christina tried the door. It was still open. The bouncer filled the frame. He waved Christina in but pointed for Zoey to get lost.

Christina said to me, "I'll see you inside, yeah?"

"Maybe."

"Definitely," Zoey corrected me. "You were obviously having a good time."

"No, I wasn't."

Christina scoffed. "You weren't? You sure kissed like you were."

I focused on Zoey. "We were just talking and then—"

Zoey clicked her tongue. "Yeah, I saw. You don't have to lie about it."

"Okay," said Christina, "this just got way too complicated. I'm going back in."

I didn't even look at her. I just heard the door slam.

"*She* kissed *me*," I told Zoey. "Not the other way around."

Zoey didn't say anything. She was sitting on the ground, hugging her knees to her chest. Just beneath the surface of her skin, her bruise was a pool of yellow.

"It looks pretty bad. Maybe you should at least see a doctor."

She didn't look at me. "You know what *fubar* means? Not the stupid name of a bar. Like the *actual word*."

"Is it Chinese or something?"

Zoey laughed like I was two. "It's an *acronym*, and I'd say it fits pretty good right now."

"What's it stand for?"

"They spelt it wrong here. It's supposed to be *fubar*, with a *u*. F-U-B-A-R. In World War Two, when things got so bad the people fighting knew they were gonna die and there was nothing they could do about it, they'd say, '*This is fubar.*' My dad used to say it all the time when I was growing up. After Mom left, he ditched the acronym. Now he usually just says the whole thing. *Fucked Up Beyond All Recognition*. Fubar. Get it?" She rubbed her hand up and down the bruise. "I think I finally understand what he means by that."

"I'm sorry," I said.

"You think you're my boyfriend?"

"No," I sputtered. "Well, I dunno. I just thought the bouncer would listen to me if he thought I wasn't just some random guy who—"

"So you were lying when you said that just now?"

"*No!* I just said it. It just came out."

"Because of last night?"

"Maybe."

"Well, we're not."

"Okay."

"We hung out. It was fun. That's all," she said. "Besides, you really want me to believe *she* kissed *you*?"

"She did!"

"Yeah, I was just thinking, she looks like the sort of girl who has trouble finding guys to make out with in parking lots."

"*I'm serious*. She's a girl I used to go to school with. That's all." I was staring at her bruise. "Your arm looks pretty bad."

"Don't touch me." She pulled away from me and stood up. "She kissed me!"

"Fine. Whatever. That's not the problem. The problem is things went too fast with you and me. Now it's all messed up. Maybe even *fubar*."

"We can slow down."

"Too late. Anyway, I don't have *boyfriends*."

"I don't care about that."

"Maybe it's better if you promise me something."

"Like what?"

"Next time you see me, just tell me to screw off, okay?"

"But why?"

"Just promise."

How could I? All I could think was that it was happening again, just like with Becky. Even when I got it right—at least I *thought* I got it right—the girl was dropping me after one time.

"I can't promise that," I said.

"You should."

"I can't."

"Fine. Whatever."

Zoey stomped off while I watched. A moment later, she had vanished around the blinding-white corner of the 7-Eleven.

55. My Shain Cope Phase

That night, when I closed my eyes, the darkness was tinged the same piss-yellow colour of the bruise on Zoey's arm. I woke up in a shitty mood.

Work didn't start until three, so most of the morning, I lay around, listening to *Freudian Slap*. The soft melody of the piano; the carnival wheeze of the accordion; the skeleton clink of the drums; the keen of the cellos; and of course the apocalyptic drawl of Shain Cope's voice—all the perfect soundtrack to how I felt.

"Is that what I think it is?"

I looked up and there was Mom, standing in my doorway.

"Sorry. Too loud?"

"No, I just haven't heard this in a long time. Shain Cope, right?"

"You know him?"

"Who doesn't?"

I shrugged. "Me."

"When I was young, he was almost a household name. He probably would've been, too, eventually." The scuffed jewel case was lying on my desk. She tapped the cover with two fingers. "It upset a lot of people when he killed himself."

"He did? Oh, wait. Somebody told me, I think." That music geek from Topher's party. It was only then I remembered him.

"He shot himself in the head," Mom told me.

"Harsh."

"It was how I first heard about him. On the news. After that, everyone I knew went through a little Shain Cope phase."

"Guess I'm going through mine right now." I sat up and slid the case off my desk, staring at the creepy cover art. "Are we going to Beauhaven today?"

"Not yet." Mom waved her hand in front of her face. "I'm still a little fuzzy."

I reached over and turned the sound down on my stereo.

"Instead of worrying about me, you just keep saving and worry about *those grades.*" She came around behind me and massaged my shoulders. Her fingers had hardly any grip. It was like a back rub from a marionette. "You'll get into a good school somewhere, a million miles from here. Everything is going to turn out fine. I promise."

She must have thought I was depressed about school. "But what if I don't get in anywhere?"

"You will," she said, and then drifted out the door, down the hall and into her room. I reset the CD, playing it again from the beginning.

56. My Mantra

When I went down for my shift, Mr. Rodolfo was talking loudly to an old Asian guy in Terminator shades about how hot it was and how a big summer storm was coming. He was standing near the front window with his arms folded, as if he was waiting for me to show up.

"I pay you enough, right?"

"Sure," I said, stepping behind the counter. "I'm doing good."

"You're saving enough?"

"I'll be good by the end of summer. Then I'll talk to my mom. It'll work out."

"Good. So you're happy."

"Yep."

"Because if you need some extra cash, I might be able to help out."

"Um ..."

"Maybe we'll talk about this later."

Then he was gone. It was an odd way of saying goodbye. I had never known him to worry about paying me enough. I couldn't help wondering if it had something to do with what happened to B-Man. Mr. Rodolfo had been acting weird ever since that morning I found the die. Did he suspect what I suspected? Was this his way of offering to pay me off?

In my head, I kept repeating the same things, over and over: *Make your goal. Make it to the end of summer. B-Man's fine. Nothing happened to him. He's fine.*

I kept repeating the words all through my shift, as the DIYers came and went, as the sun set on Steinway. At some point, maybe simply out of mental fatigue, my thoughts shifted. They leapt from B-Man to Zoey. Would I ever see her again? I didn't think so. When someone says, "Next time you see me, promise you'll tell me to screw off," you don't expect them to show up on your doorstep the next day.

But that night, just before closing, that's what she did.

57. The Importance of Being Honest

She stopped on the threshold of the laundromat, the rattler slung over her shoulder.

"Is your boss here?" she whispered.

"No."

I didn't feel like talking, but I couldn't take my eyes off her. Her dreads were pulled back in a tight ponytail. It gave the edges of her face an added sharpness.

"I can trust you, right?"

"Of course."

"I mean, you're an honest person."

I nodded. She looked back over her shoulder. The light was fading by the second. The summer storm was coming.

"Seriously," she said, "you've always been *honest* with me, yeah?"

I threw out this deep, theatrical sigh. "I have no idea why you're asking me this, but *yes*."

"And you're honest with everyone, right?"

"I just told you—*yes*. I have always been honest with you. I'm honest with everyone. *Okay?*"

"I'm serious, Kaz. It's important." She looked back over her shoulder again. "I need someone I can trust right now."

"Are you in trouble?"

She ran her thumb and forefinger up and down one of the instrument's strings. It made a noise like a whine, like the whimper of an animal before it died. "I need you to stash this for me."

"Where am I supposed to put it?"

She pointed at the dry-cleaning booth. "In there. Like before."

"What if my boss comes back? I would definitely lose my job."

"Is that all you care about? Your job?"

"That's not true."

She came inside, leaning the rattler against the counter. "Just for a couple hours. I don't have anyone else."

"Wait, you never answered me. Are you in trouble?"

"They're gonna take it," she said.

"*Who's* gonna take it?"

She looked out the window again. I noticed another bruise on the side of her neck. She was wearing a white, gauzy, long-sleeved shirt, and I thought I could see the bruise spreading down her back.

"What happened to your neck?"

"It's from carrying the rattler all the time." She pulled the elastic out of her hair. Her dreads tumbled down to cover the bruise. "Probably looks worse cuz I had to run with it just now."

"*Run?* Why? What's going on?"

"You're right. I'm kind of in trouble."

"With who?"

"If I tell you, will you let me stash it here? Just a couple hours, I promise."

"Fine. Who are you in trouble with?"

"The police."

"The cops?" Now I was the one peering anxiously out the window. "What did you do?"

"Nothing," she said. "They said I needed a permit to perform, which is total bullshit. It's like five hundred bucks for a busker's licence, but the fine's even worse. So I hoofed it. If they arrest me, they'll impound the rattler. *Who knows* when I'll get it back."

"Okay, just a couple hours."

"*Great!*" Her face brightened and she leaned across the counter, pecking me on the cheek. It happened so fast, I didn't have a chance to turn my head and make it a real kiss. Even still, it felt good.

"We close at ten," I told her. "You gotta be back by then."

"I will. I promise."

58. Not All Promises Are Created Equal

The rain started just after eight. First, that humid, earthy, before-the-rain smell wafted through the open door. Then, all at once, the whole sky thundered and flashed and fell down in sheets. Water rushed through the gutters of Steinway, carrying pop cans and candy wrappers like bits of a shipwreck.

Maybe Zoey was caught in the rain somewhere. I pictured her in my head, her dreads sopping down the sides of her face. I texted her:

U ok?

No answer.

For an hour, the rain came and went before finally letting up. The streets were soaked and Zoey's "couple hours" were up, but there was no sign of her. I sent another text:

Gotta close in 1 hr. Txt me, pls.

No reply.

At ten, I locked up the laundromat and flipped the OPEN sign to CLOSED. I didn't switch off the lights. I slumped on the bench by the front window and moped at the drying pavement. Zoey would show up any minute, I figured, appearing like magic, like she always did.

Only she didn't. I waited for an hour with the lights on.

Where ARE you?

Nothing.

The rattler was tucked away in the same place as before, deep in the back of the dry-cleaning booth. Only the bottom was visible, the base extending down below the clothes. I began to worry. Either she had been arrested or she had lied to me. Otherwise, she would be here. Around eleven-thirty, I texted one last rant.

I hope ur ok, but u need to tell me if u cant get back. I'll keep the rattler til noon 2mrrow … after that, I might hafta trash it. OK?

I waited. I kept hearing her promise in my head. Why did she have to promise? I waited and waited for a reply but there was …

Nothing.

59. S.C.

I put a crate of detergent in the dry-cleaning booth. From the counter, you couldn't see the rattler. I had the morning shift the next day, so it should be all right in there. But I remembered how Mr. Rodolfo and the Brothers had shown up unexpectedly on the morning I found B-Man's die. If that happened again, I'd be in trouble.

It was hard sleeping again; I was too worried. If Zoey didn't come in the morning, what would I do with the rattler? Thankfully, the Sit'N'Spin was dark and empty when I finally went down the next day. I texted Zoey again:

Still have your instrument. WHERE ARE YOU?

No answer.

I started to wonder if I could truly follow through on my threat to trash the instrument. A part of me wanted to. After all that stuff about being "an honest person," Zoey had basically lied to me. She promised she'd be back and never showed.

It was a slow morning. The street felt deserted. I folded towels; I stacked the little boxes of detergent; I swept the floor.

Mostly, I stood behind the counter like a zombie, staring out the window, waiting for Zoey to walk in.

Instead of Zoey, a crimson convertible pulled up across the street, the one that belonged to the TV producer, Andrew Myers. He got out, looking even more glamorous than I remembered. As he came across the street, the sun glinted off his car like flashbulbs along a red carpet.

"You got those suits for me?" he asked, breezing in the door.

"Oh, yeah," I said, like a complete kiss-up. "Totally done!"

In my head, an impossible fantasy went spinning out of control: Andrew Myers telling me he liked my "look"; Andrew Myers casting me in his next big flick; Andrew Myers asking me to direct the sequel. There was even room in there for Zoey. (I would hire her to score the soundtrack.) A whole, sparkling lifetime unfolded behind my eyes, all in the few steps Andrew Myers took from the door to the counter.

"How's the shoot going?" I asked him, stifling my excitement. "Sorry, it's Andrew, right?"

"You remembered. Cool." He smiled and his teeth glittered as brightly as the hood of his car. "It's going pretty good. Like I said, right now it's mostly second unit stuff, no biggie."

Inside the dry-cleaning booth, I had to move the crate of detergent to get to where I'd hung his suits. I plucked them off the bar and they crackled in their plastic sheaths.

"Here you go."

"Great, how much do I owe you?" His wallet was thick as a brick of butter.

Each suit cost fifteen, but he paid me twenty. "Call it a tip, for getting it done on time—and for remembering my name."

"Thanks!" I popped open the cash, slid in the price of the suits and pocketed the rest. When I looked up again, Myers was staring into the dry-cleaning booth. I had left the door open.

"What's that?" he asked me.

"It's where we keep the dry cleaning."

"No." He came around the counter and pushed the door open all the way. "I mean *that*, right there." He was pointing at the rattler, partly exposed by the gap left by Myers's clothes.

"Just some old junk," I told him.

He stepped fully inside the booth, shoving the hanging clothes aside. "No way," he said, speaking quietly, more to himself than me. "It can't be."

"Can't be what?"

"Oh my god. How did it get here?"

"I told you, it's just some old junk. A friend of mine made it."

He shook his head. "I don't think so."

"What do you mean?"

"Whoever your friend is, there's no way he made this."

"*She.*"

Myers ignored me. He went inside and crouched down in front of the instrument. He ran the pad of his thumb along one of the strings. It gave off an eerie, faraway whine, a sour version of a sound I recognized.

"She wouldn't like you touching it," I told him.

Very gently, Myers lifted his fingers from the string. He stood up and faced me. "Did you *see* her make it?"

"No, but I've seen her play it. She's really good."

He bit his lip. "So she's had it a long time."

"What are you talking about?"

"I guarantee, your friend didn't make this."

"How do you know that?"

"I think I can prove it. Help me get it out on the counter."

I didn't move. It was the middle of the morning. What if Mr. Rodolfo came in early? I couldn't have that thing splayed out on the counter.

"I'll do it myself." He reached past the clothes and picked up the instrument. "You're gonna want to see this."

I just stood there, too stunned to speak. When Myers came out of the booth, a puff of stale air came with him. It smelled of chemicals and plastic. I felt dizzy.

Myers eased the rattler onto the counter. "*See?* C'mere and look." He tapped the bottom of the base. "I can't believe it!"

The centre strut of the rattler was made of polished wood, but the bottom was capped with dull grey metal, pocked and pitted from countless thumps against pavement.

"See that?"

Myers had found two scratches that were deeper than the rest. That's because they weren't scratches. They had been carved there deliberately. Two letters, underlined with a little flourish:

S.C.

"What's it mean?"

"It means your friend lied to you."

"About what?"

"Did she ever tell you where she got this?"

"She said she made it herself." I explained as much as I knew, which suddenly seemed like very little: that Zoey had constructed it out of scraps of junk; that it was her own design for a musical instrument; that although she was good at all kinds of instruments, she preferred to play her own. "So it *has* to be hers—because she can play it. Look at it! Who else could play something like this?"

"Only one person I know." Myers tapped the letters. "S.C.," he said. "Shain Cope."

If I felt dizzy before, now I was close to passing out. I had that same feeling I got whenever I saw blood, like my insides were floating away. I gripped the edge of the counter to stop it from happening.

"I don't … I don't get it."

"It's simple," said Myers. "This instrument doesn't belong to your friend."

"It doesn't?"

"She *certainly* didn't make it, because *Shain Cope* did." He pursed his lips at me. "Kid, this instrument was stolen."

"No. You've never heard her play it. If you had, you'd know." I pointed out the window. "She stands right over there and she plays it. *She kills it.* Every time. I've seen her. She's amazing!"

Myers stared into my face. Suddenly, he smiled. "Oh, I get it. She's cute, isn't she? She's not just 'a friend.'" He leaned a bit closer. "Just cuz she's cute doesn't mean she's honest."

There was that word again. *Honest.* If Zoey had been lying to me since the beginning, how could she have grilled me like that, asking all those questions?

"I've seen her," I whispered. "She kills it."

Andrew Myers shrugged. "Maybe. But so did Shain Cope. *And* it's a well-known fact he made his own instruments. It's what he was famous for. He used to joke in interviews, say that someday he was gonna make the world's *greatest instrument.* One time, he said that if he ever finished the thing, he'd have nothing left to live for. That was one reason it was such a big deal when he killed himself. Nobody knew what it meant. They all wanted to know: Had he done it? Had he succeeded?"

We both stared at the instrument. It suddenly looked different to me, like something in a morgue. A rotten body on a slab.

"How do you know all this?"

"I was a fan," he said. "I still am. Also, in case you hadn't noticed, I'm a little older than you. For some people of my generation, Shain Cope was a god. Plus, I live in LA. Everybody out there knows the story." He nodded, remembering. "After he killed himself, after the news got out, some people broke into his house in the Hills. They stole the usual stuff: electronics, jewellery, anything that looked valuable. It was only after a complete inventory that they discovered there were other things missing. Instruments. *Homemade instruments*. Eventually, nearly all of it was recovered. All except *one thing*." He placed a hand on the rattler. "They said it was the last instrument he made before he died, and there was a rumour about it."

"What rumour?"

"That it was shaped like a cross."

My head was swimming again (drowning, more like).

"Are you saying my, um—my friend … *She stole this?*"

"I'm saying she's gonna have to do some serious explaining, maybe to some very serious people."

I thought about the night before. Was this what Zoey was running from? Was this the *real reason* the cops were after her?

"So now what? Are you going to call the police?"

He laughed, a few short blasts, almost like he was choking. "That's the *last* thing I need."

"So you're *not* going to call them?"

He leaned even closer, his head hovering over the strings. "Listen," he said, lowering his voice. "Maybe this is your lucky day. Not everyone would recognize what this is. And maybe—yeah—some people would call the cops. But here's the thing: I'm a collector."

"So …?"

He took a deep breath. "I know this thing isn't yours, but I also know it's *definitely not* your friend's. So what would you say if I asked you to sell it to me?"

"*What?*"

"If you're worried about your friend, you can split the money with her."

"I don't know. I'd have to ask her first."

The gleam in Myers's eyes had shifted from a movie-star twinkle to something else, something more like the glint of a blade. "What if I wanted to buy it right now? I'm willing to pay a lot of money."

"It's not mine."

He cleared his throat and stood up straight. He could probably tell he was making me nervous. He was.

"Look, I'm only in town a few more days, and I'd really like to take this off your hands. You see what I mean?"

"I don't know."

"Let me put it another way, because I don't think you understand. Whoever your friend is, I'd be doing her *a big favour.*" He pointed to the instrument. "This is stolen property. Now, I don't know if she's the one who stole it, but somehow she got it and she's been lying about where it came from." He threw a glance into the dry-cleaning booth. "And it looks to me like you've been stashing it for her. So all I'm saying is that you could both be in a lot of trouble." He turned back to me, a sympathetic expression on his face. "Sell it to me right now and all that goes away."

This must be how you got movies made, by saying the right thing at just the right time. I could feel how badly Myers wanted it. Something about the intensity of his need made me want to keep it—at least for now. What it made me want most of all was to talk to Zoey, to hear her tell me the truth.

"No. I can't. I need to talk to her."

Myers touched the rattler again. "Okay, well, you tell your friend there's a guy who knows what this thing is, and you tell her he doesn't care where she got it but he wants it. *Very badly.*" He took another business card out of his wallet. "This one's for her. You tell her I'll be in town until Monday."

"Wait," I said. "She'll want to know what you'll give her for it."

He shrugged. "How 'bout fifty?"

I couldn't believe it. After everything he just said, I almost laughed. "That's it? Fifty bucks?"

Myers threw his head back and belted out another gunshot whoop of laughter.

"Not fifty bucks. *Fifty thousand bucks.*"

60. The Three Words That Played on Repeat inside My Head for Hours after Andrew Myers Left

Fifty! Thousand! Dollars!

61. A Sampling of Unanswered Texts I Sent to Zoey That Morning

Seriously, my boss gets here @ 12:30 LATEST. your thing cannot b here!!

what if i had a way 4 u to go to any music school you wanted? would u txt me then?

WHERE R U???

should i b worried?

you cud at least answer me

ok, so I'm worried now. PLS call or txt.

That's it. I cant w8. My boss'll be here. im moving the thing upstairs. txt me when u come to get it.

62. A Surprise Gift

"What's *that?*" Nomi asked as soon as I was inside the entranceway.

"It's nothing," I lied. "Just a thing."

Nomi ran for a closer look but then stopped. "Are those ... *bones?*"

"Shh, you'll wake Mom."

"She's in her room but I don't think she's asleep."

"Well, don't tell her about this. It's a surprise."

Nomi stared wide-eyed at the rattler. "You bought that for her? Like a present?"

"It's an antique. Really valuable." At least that much was true.

Nomi wasn't convinced. "Looks like a whole bunch of garbage to me."

"It's a musical instrument." I tugged on one of the strings and got a shivering note. "You know how before you were born, when Dad was alive, we used to have a real piano?"

Nomi hung her head. "Yeah, I know. But now it's gone."

"I thought Mom might like something new. There's no

room for a piano, so …" I shifted the rattler on my shoulder. The bones rung lightly together. Nomi nodded, but after a moment's thought, she looked on the verge of tears.

"What's wrong?"

"I didn't get her anything!" she said, her voice starting to crack.

"No, it's cool. This is from both of us."

"It is?"

"Help me take it to my room. We'll hide it under my bed, but quick, I gotta get back to work."

Nomi kept the chains and cogs from rattling and we carried it down the hall. It nearly fit under my bed, with just the bottom sticking out. The initials were carved clearly into the bottom. *S.C.* I covered it with my gym bag.

"When are we going to give it to her?" Nomi asked.

I had to think about this. After Zoey and I sold it to Andrew Myers, I would have to explain to Nomi why it had suddenly disappeared. I could already hear her questions. *What happened to Mom's present? Where did it go?* Then again, once we sold it, we'd have so much money, no one would care. I could buy Nomi her very own violin. That ought to cheer her up.

"Let's wait until Mom's feeling a bit better," I said. "Maybe after she goes to Beauhaven."

Nomi agreed. "She always feels better after she goes there."

I hadn't been upstairs for long, but when I returned to the Sit'N'Spin, I knew I was in trouble. Mr. Rodolfo was there, arms folded, red faced, standing behind the counter. A trio of DIYers crowded around, shrugging in bewilderment as he interrogated them about something. I had a hunch he was grilling them about where I was.

"*There* he is!" Mr. Rodolfo shouted, pointing at me with

the flat of his hand. "You might as well turn around and leave. *You're fired!*"

"I just needed to go upstairs for like, *one sec*, because—"

"*No-no-no!*" Mr. Rodolfo shook an angry finger at me. "No excuses! This is a *business* establishment." He pointed to the till. "What were you thinking? There's *money* in here, you understand?"

"I just …" A new and perfect lie popped into my head. "It's my mom. She came back from the hospital and she needed something."

Mr. Rodolfo paused to look up at the ceiling. "She okay?"

"She is now."

"Good, because we're not finished here." He pointed a thumb backward over his shoulder. "I want to talk to you."

"Where?"

"Downstairs."

He turned and led the way, not bothering to see if I followed. He took the stairs sideways, his shoulders rolling heavily with each step. Why had I never noticed that before? He lumbered downstairs like an old bear.

The door to his office was locked. He opened it up and ushered me into the room I'd seen a few days earlier.

"Have a seat, Kaz."

I sat in one of the plastic chairs.

"I'm only going to ask you this once, okay?"

"I told you, my mom's sick. I had to bring her something."

Mr. Rodolfo shut his eyes. "It's not that."

"So what is it?"

"Are you trying to steal from me?"

"*What?*"

"Don't lie, Kaz. It's too late for that."

"I would never, *ever* steal from you."

"But you *would* let your freaky girlfriend contaminate the shop? Is that it? Because even if you'd never steal from me, I'm pretty sure *she* would."

"She? Who?"

"The Jesus freak," he said, making a face. "I know you put that thing in with the dry cleaning. I saw you."

How? I thought.

"What if one of my customers gets some disease?" He shook his head. "Talk about bad for business!"

I was still speechless. I had made sure we were alone when we hid the rattler. How could he know?

"Is that why you tried to break in here? Into my office? Did she ask you to steal from me?"

"No!" He knew about me coming down here. *How?* In a tiny, sullen voice I said, "Zoey isn't like that."

"What do you know?" He looked at me like I was a worm, like I had no brain to top off my rubbery spine. "Why do you think that door was open when you came down here, snooping around like a thief? I *left* it open. It was a *test*, you get it? I wanted to see what you'd do."

My head was spinning, again. The *whole room* was spinning.

"Wait, how do you know I came down here?"

"In here."

He pushed out his chair and went to the other door in the corner, the one I had knocked on just before Andrew Myers showed up. When he opened it, I saw that it was nearly empty. The only thing inside was another shelving unit, full of old video recorders. I knew what the blinking red lights meant.

"You're recording," I whispered.

"Me and my brothers installed them a couple weeks ago."

He pointed to a shiny grey dome, hanging from the corner of the ceiling. "So many weirdos coming around. I never thought you'd be one of them."

He pressed a button on one of the recorders and flicked on the old TV on top of the filing cabinet. The screen showed a black-and-white image of upstairs. There I was—with Zoey—on the night of our date at What the Pho? We were carrying the rattler into the dry-cleaning booth.

"I don't get it," Mr. Rodolfo said. "Why'd you wanna bring that in here?"

"It wasn't for long."

He pointed at the screen. "I can't believe you let a freak like that in here."

"She's *not* a freak! She's just …" What was she, really? I didn't know anymore.

"You gonna tell me what you were looking for down here?"

"I was just …" How could I tell him the truth? How could I tell him I was checking to see where he had hidden B-Man's body? Obviously, it wasn't down here. "I was just curious."

"Good, you can get curious about finding another job."

"Fine then," I said, and I meant it. I was sick of Mr. Rodolfo, the way he wrote people off just because of how they looked. I was sick of how obsessed he was with running his shitty little business—a dead-end laundromat in fucking Evandale. I was especially sick of how the whole world got cleaved down the middle: good for business and bad for business.

Of course, it was easy not to give a shit about your job when these three little words kept marching through my head:

Fifty!
Thousand!
Dollars!

63. Ten Million Hits in 0.15 Seconds

I needed to find Zoey, but she wasn't answering her phone. I texted her for the zillionth time.

Please call me. I have good news.

Upstairs, Nomi wondered what I was doing back so soon. I told her I had the day off. In my room, I pulled out the rattler. The initials stared me in the face.

S. C.

What if I sold the rattler *without* telling Zoey? How could she mind, especially if I split the money with her? With that kind of cash, she could buy a whole orchestra. Better than that, she could fly off to whatever music school she wanted. Anyway, the rattler—or whatever it was really called—wasn't even hers in the first place.

Then again, the thought of her on a plane gave me a stab of regret, and I knew if I sold the instrument without telling her, she would hate me.

On the other hand, *it was* just *so much money*.

That got me thinking. If Andrew Myers was willing to

shell out *Fifty! Thousand! Dollars!* for a long-lost Shain Cope instrument, maybe he knew something I didn't. Maybe it was worth even more.

I googled "rood rattler," but nothing came up. It was probably a name Zoey made up. Shain Cope could have dubbed it something completely different, so I searched for the man himself. There were *ten million hits.*

I went through fan sites, lyrics, Wikipedia entries, grainy videos of live performances, zillions of photographs, many of which featured strange, otherworldly instruments, but nothing that looked like what was under my bed.

It was odd to see so many images of the man. Generally, I didn't give much thought to the CDs Dave Mizra brought over. Some were good, some weren't; but Shain Cope was different. In every way. The singer's ghost was haunting every aspect of my life.

In the pictures, he was perpetually shy, always looking away from the camera, rarely granting the photographer a clear view of his face. Getting his features steady in your mind was like piecing together a puzzle, shifting the angles from different images. His strong jaw and a jutting brow gave him a slightly concave face. He heightened the effect with a grisly pompadour and matching goatee. It made him look only half human. On-stage, his teeth gleaming as he sang, he was more like a wild animal, a starving wolf.

Cope's Wikipedia page said he was known "not only for his distinctive, rumbling voice but also for constructing his own instruments, several of which he used on his final, most famous album, *Freudian Slap.*" I learned that no one saw it coming when he shot himself. He didn't leave a suicide note. Later, probably because his house was empty and his death was so well publicized, there was a break-in. A link sent me to a scanned newspaper article published that same summer:

The vacant home of idiosyncratic musician Shain Cope, who took his own life in April, was last night the site of an opportunistic robbery. Thieves gained entrance through a ground-floor window some time before three o'clock in the morning, making off with a number of valuables.

"This was a heinous, cynical crime," said Los Feliz chief of police Raymond Saunders. "These are criminals who took advantage of a man's death to enrich themselves, acting at a time when his family was already dealing with so much pain."

Local authorities would not specify what had been stolen, but Cope's mother, Eleanor, confirmed that at least one of her son's most valuable instruments is currently missing. "It's really the only thing we want back," she said.

"It was so much a part of who he was."

Cope's career as a singer-songwriter began in 1970 with the release of his critically acclaimed debut album *Four Lane Road*. By the end of the decade, he had proven himself not only as a musician, but also as a gifted craftsman, designing and building the unusual instruments that gave him his unique sound. Among these were a steam-powered organ and a multi-storey drum kit made from the engines of classic cars. Although the value of the stolen articles is unknown, all of Cope's pieces were one of a kind. Their value is thought to be considerable.

Shain Cope died of a self-inflicted gunshot wound on April 18, 1983. His ashes were scattered to the Pacific Ocean by friends and family, in accordance with his wishes.

After reading the article, I wanted to hear the music again. I put on some headphones, shut my eyes and listened. I wanted to see if I could hear it. The rattler.

I did.

The hollow chinks of bones and chains. The rough whine of a bow chafing over taut strings. Thumps like a felled tree come to life, trying to stab itself back into the earth. In my head, I saw Shain Cope, a howling wolf-man, clawing at the very same instrument that now lay dead on my bedroom carpet.

When the final strains of "Get Me Home" faded, I lay there in the dark. I thought about all the places Zoey had lived. Europe, Mexico City, Montreal, New York, California. *LA was crazy*, she had said. What did that mean? The rest were just names of places, but LA—she had paused when she mentioned LA. *LA was crazy*. But no, Zoey wouldn't have even been born in 1983. But there were those times her voice sounded so old. *How old?* I had never asked her.

No, I thought, it was impossible. Anyone could see she was my age, or at least somewhere in the ballpark. Even if she was one or two years older—even *five* years older—there was no way she could have robbed an LA mansion *in 1983*. So how did she get it? The question hung in my head, words coiling like smoke above a dark stage, one where Shain Cope had just folded his last bow.

My phone buzzed.

What good news? z

64. Oceans of Applause

"Mom?"

She was in the kitchen by the window, staring out at nothing. This newest attack, coming so quickly after the last one, had really taken its toll. I was completely ready to drive her up to Beaumont, if only it would make her feel better.

"Mom?"

"Uh-huh?"

"There's someone here to see me."

"Who?"

"A friend."

"Calen?"

"Somebody else. She just needs to pick up some stuff. It'll only take a second."

Mom blinked at me. *"She?"*

"Just a girl I know. I have something of hers. She'll only be here for five minutes, okay?"

She turned back to the window, sizing herself up in the reflection. "Can I meet her?" she asked, smoothing her hair.

It struck me as an odd request; Mom hated seeing people after an attack. "Are you sure?"

"Just bring her up."

Out on the street, Zoey looked amazing. The setting sun turned her skin to gold and she was dressed in the same clothes she wore the first time I saw her. The same cut-off jeans; the same T-shirt, still melting off her shoulder; the same pink bra. A few dreads hung across her face like a shredded veil.

She frowned when I came out empty-handed. "Where is it?" she asked. "You still have it, right?"

"Where have you been? How come you never answered any of my texts?"

"I was in *trouble*," she said, as if that was explanation enough. "Have you got it?"

"It's upstairs."

"So are you gonna bring it down?"

"Could you come up a sec? There's something I want to ask you."

Her whole body twitched. "Ask me here."

"Just come up. Anyway, you look hungry. You can have something to eat if you want."

"I don't need food. I just need—"

"My mom said she wants to meet you."

"She did?"

"Just come up, okay?"

Mom was still at the window, still staring out. "Hello there," she greeted Zoey, who came in behind me. "You're a friend of Kaz's?"

"Uh-huh."

"What's your name?"

"Zoey."

"That's nice." She tilted her head and pointed a finger at Zoey. "I think I know who you are."

Zoey's eyes flashed. "How?"

"I've seen you. Across the street."

Zoey shrugged. "I play there sometimes."

"You're very good," Mom said.

Zoey tugged a couple more of her dreads in front of her face. "Thanks."

Nomi came to the kitchen door, but stopped on the threshold, hugging the door frame. Zoey obviously freaked her out a bit.

Mom was silent, too. She was thinking about something, staring oddly at Zoey. "I dreamed about you," she said.

Zoey made a noise like something was stuck in her throat. "You *dreamed* about me?"

"You were beside the sea. You were playing your instrument, only it was falling to pieces. But you still played beautifully. Even the waves clapped. They went *psh-psh-psh* against the sand. A whole ocean, cheering for you."

Zoey had no idea what to say to that. Who would?

"It's a pleasure to meet you," Mom said. She reached out with a limp hand and Zoey took it.

"Nice to meet you, too."

Nomi was gone when we turned to leave the kitchen. In my room, the first thing Zoey said was, "Your mom's kind of … odd."

"She's not feeling well."

"No offence, but I think that's an understatement."

"She's just tired."

"Well, anyway, I like her. She's nice. Weird, but nice." Zoey took in a quick survey of the room. "Okay. So where is it?"

"Hold on," I said. I had carefully replaced my dirty laundry, covering the rattler where it protruded from under the bed. "Can I ask you something?"

"What?"

"Would you ever sell it?"

"Yeah, right."

"Really?"

"Never."

"You're sure?"

"Is this it over here, under your bed?" She poked her toe into my clothes, finding the base.

"What if I could get you a lot of money for it? Like, *loads* of money."

"Not everyone cares about money, you know." She picked away the dirty clothes. The rattler's chains clinked on the floor. "This isn't something you can just sell. You *wouldn't believe* how long it took me to make it."

"Oh, yeah?" My voice came out with an edge. "How long would you say?"

She shrugged. "I dunno, a long time."

"About how long?"

"It wasn't like I was punching a clock. I can't remember *exactly.*" She pulled the rattler all the way out, propping it against the wall. "I made it years ago."

"Did you really?"

Her eyes narrowed at me. "What's that supposed to mean?"

"It's just a question." I was getting angry. All I wanted was to hear the truth. "You really made it?"

"*Yes.* And it took a long time." She was looking at the instrument, not me. "A couple years, maybe. Y'know, to get it to sound right."

It was so obvious she was lying. Why hadn't I seen it before?

"Maybe you'd understand," she said, turning back at me with a look of disgust, "if you could actually make something, instead of just fold towels."

That hurt, especially because I knew she was lying. I almost wanted to grab the thing and toss it out the window. But instead, very calmly, I said, "Two years, huh?"

"Yeah, about that. Two years."

"And you won't sell it? Not even if I told you I knew someone who'd pay a ton for it?"

"Like who?"

"Maybe I know somebody."

She sighed. "You don't get it, do you? All you think about is money. It's not like that for me. It's about the *who*, not the *how much*. I'd only sell it to someone I trusted, someone special to me. Somebody who would take care of it—*and play it*. That's what it's made for."

"Am I special to you?"

"You were. I don't know, maybe you still are. It's confusing." She stared at me with her big, glittering eyes and I almost changed my mind.

Almost.

"Let me buy it off you."

She laughed. "*You?* Why would you even want it?"

"It's not for me," I said—exactly the same as I had lied to Nomi. "It's for my mom."

Zoey didn't understand.

"You saw her. She gets depressed sometimes. And you heard what she said. She *dreamed* about you." If Zoey wouldn't tell me the truth, then I could spin my own lies. "When I was a kid, she played in an orchestra, and when she saw you playing, she told me she wished she could have it. She said it would finally get her playing again. Don't you get it? It's not just you she dreams about. She dreams about this, the rattler. And you said it yourself, it needs to be played."

"She wants to play it?"

"You can always build another one. Right?" Zoey nodded slowly, but she seemed unsure. "It'd have to be a *shitload* of money. Music schools aren't cheap."

I felt a jab of triumph. I had got her to admit it. Money mattered to her, just as much as it did to me.

"Okay," I said. "How much do you want?"

"It depends. How much have you got?"

65. The Last Time I Saw Her, Part 1

The last time I saw Zoey Zamani, she was boarding a streetcar. The doors clapped shut and the iron wheels went slicing east along Steinway. When she took her seat, she didn't look out through the glass. She just sat there, sitting on top of my whole life. That's because in her back pocket, there were twenty-two personal cheques, each one for $500 and all signed by me. That's how Zoey wanted it. She said it would save her some hassle. If it was all on a single cheque, it would be difficult to cash it.

Twenty-two little rectangles of paper. It was everything I had.

When the streetcar vanished over the rise, I went straight back upstairs and called the number on Andrew Myers's business card. There was no answer. I waited for a messaging service to click in, but it never did. I hung up and tried again. This time, he picked up before the second ring.

"Yeah? Myers." His voice was slower and gruffer than before, as if he had just flopped out of bed.

"Mr. Myers?"

"Make it quick." He cleared his throat and his voice slid

back to the smoothness I remembered. "We're just about to roll."

"It's Kaz Barrett." I started explaining who I was, but he cut in before I finished.

"*Oh, kid!* Sure, I remember who you are. You talk to your friend? You got some good news for me?"

"I do. I've got it right here. The instrument."

"That's great!"

"So can you come and get it? I'm ready to sell it to you."

"Yes! Totally! But not *right* this instant. I'm with the crew until late tonight, so ..." He paused to think. I heard indistinct chatter in the background, the rush of wind, or maybe traffic. "Okay, what about tomorrow, lunchtime? I'll come by the laundromat. Sound okay?"

"Uh, no. Not there." I didn't think he needed to know I'd been fired, but I also didn't want him coming to the apartment. "Better if we meet across the street. There's a jewellery shop there called Mizra's Fire & Ice."

"Sorry, where?"

"It's right where you parked last time."

"I park a lot of places."

"It's directly across from the laundromat. You can't miss it." I had him write down the name, just in case. "Meet me there at twelve noon."

After I hung up, I felt relieved. The arrangements were made. But I also had an awful feeling like I'd never see Zoey again. When I put her on that streetcar, what I remembered most was the look of disappointment on her face. It was as if, in some deep and unthinkable way, I had failed her.

66. A Bit of Blue Sky

To clear my head, I went for a walk. I ended up in Montgomery Park, where the skinny guy in the straw hat was still there, still hawking his photographs of crumbling cathedrals.

"See anything you like?" There was a slight whistle to his S. It came from a black hole in the middle of his grin. All his front teeth were missing.

"Just passing through."

"Look all you want, won't cost a dime, but stand there for too long and I start charging rent!"

I gave the guy a half-hearted laugh.

"Where's that?" I asked, pointing to the only colour photograph on the blanket. It was a view from below of a crumbling wall of red and brown bricks. The only break from the pitted surface was a single bullet-shaped window, high in the corner. Through it, you could see a patch of clouds and blue sky.

"Just a stop along the way," said the guy, unhelpfully. "Probably not there anymore. Would'ja believe they're gonna level the place for condos?"

"It's a nice picture."

"Like it enough to buy it?"

Maybe, I thought, *but not yet.* The picture summed up how I felt: hemmed in by the walls of Evandale, but with a bright flicker of blue sky up in some far-off corner.

"Not right now," I told the guy behind the blanket, "but maybe later. I've got a very big paycheque coming tomorrow."

"Good for you. Just make sure you come find me when your ship comes in."

I was walking away, almost out of earshot, when I heard the guy call to someone else.

"Yo, B! Where's Razor at?"

I spun around and there he was. The whole time I'd been gawking at photographs, he had been sitting right behind me, flopped on a park bench.

B-Man.

"Oh my god! You're alive."

B-Man shrugged as if he wasn't sure. "I'm alive."

"Where have you *been?*"

"Aw …" He looked nervously up and down the street.

I sat down beside him and regretted it immediately. He smelled terrible.

"What happened?"

He shook his head. "Don't wanna talk about it!"

"Talk about what?"

He winced, pulling his lips back like a snarling dog, but the effect wasn't fierce. It wasn't the glare of a wild animal. It made him look frightened. "You see A-Man?" he asked me.

"Not for a few days."

B-Man shut his eyes tight. His teeth did the same, all

gnashed together. "I lost it. Don't know where it is. Or else *they* stole it. Somebody stole it! Anyhow, I can't find it, because …
aw, I'll *never* find it."

This was the part when I usually phased out, the part when B-Man flew off to his private planet of jibber-jabber. This time, I didn't ignore him. "You mean your die, don't you?"

B-Man nodded like a child without a toy. My hand was already in my pocket, about to get out the die, when he said, "It don't matter."

"How come?"

"Because *nothing* does. Get it?"

"No. I don't."

Suddenly, B-Man started to cry. Huge, kick-ass, full body sobs. The perimeter of people around us widened. That was them doing what I used to do, ignoring him. It was probably like that for B-Man all the time. So even though he smelled like complete shit, I put an arm around him. Meanwhile, he just sat there with snot streaming down his lip, panting out these fast, scary-sounding breaths.

"Razor's dead!"

"What?"

"A car hit her."

And so, just like that, the little white cube in my pocket made sense. It wasn't B-Man's blood I saw, it was Razor's.

"Behind the Sit'N'Spin, right?"

B-Man was stunned enough to stop crying. "How do you know that?"

"I saw Mr. Rodolfo cleaning up the—cleaning up behind the alley."

B-Man nodded. "The guy didn't even stop. Didn't give a shit about neither of us." He spat a glob of grey spit into the grass. "That's where I been. I went up north to bury her. She liked it up north. There's a field up there I found where she could run and run all she wanted. I took a shovel up there and buried her."

"I know this might not seem like a big deal right now, but maybe it'll cheer you up a bit." I took the die out of my pocket and gave it back to him. "I found it in the alley."

"Hey, thanks."

He stared at it for a while, rolling it around his palm. "Cracked the old girl's skull wide open and just kept driving." He closed his fist and looked at me. "You see a little red convertible with a big dent in the front, you do me a favour and slash the tires, scratch the paint, I don't care, just fuck it up."

"A red convertible?"

"That's what did it."

How many shiny red convertibles were there in Evandale? Andrew Myers had probably killed Razor. Why would a movie producer slow down to save the life of a homeless guy's dog?

I decided I would give some of the money to B-Man. If he wanted to go out and buy a thousand little dice, he could. If he wanted to get himself a new, equally stinky mutt, I would help him find one.

"Don't worry," I said. "Things'll turn out okay. You'll see."

B-Man didn't believe me. He turned his puffy, sunburnt, snot-streaked face away, covering his eyes with his sleeve.

"She was my pinion," he whispered.

"What?"

"My little piece of the machine."

67. Haunted

In the morning, I wrapped newspaper and blankets loosely around the rattler, fastening it all with masking tape. When I had finished, it looked very much like I'd murdered a scarecrow and was preparing to dump the body.

Mom was in her room, which was good, but Nomi was lying in front of the TV, watching the final episode of *Big Daddy*. There was no way to sneak past her, so I just went for it.

"Is that the thing for Mom?" she asked, when I moved past the doorway.

I nodded and put a finger to my lips. "Don't tell her, but there's a problem. One of the pieces? It's broken. I'm just gonna take it across the street. Dave Mizra has tools and he said he could fix it."

Nomi nodded slowly, like it all made sense, but there was something she was missing. "Why's it all wrapped up?"

"I told you, because it's broken."

"Can I see?"

"No. I'll be right back."

It hadn't rained since the storm, so the street was a blizzard of summer dust. Sand and grit and strips of paper collected in the gutter. It was five to twelve. I was right on time.

It was Sunday and Dave Mizra's shop was closed. The poster of Shain Cope hung in the shadows of the back wall. He stared out at me through spirals of cigarette smoke. I felt haunted. It didn't help that I was about to sell off what was possibly the man's most prized possession. To escape the singer's gaze, I dragged the instrument into an alcove beside the shop.

Every time something red drove past, my heart went crazy. It was always a taxi or a rusty minivan. Never a flashy convertible. By twelve fifteen, I began to worry. I called Myers's number, but—same as yesterday—there was no answer. I tried again at twelve thirty, then at one o'clock. That was when the door in the alcove behind me opened up.

"Kaz-o-matic!" It was Dave Mizra, looking pretty haggard. He was uncharacteristically dressed in a baggy grey track suit and worn sandals. Stubble sprouted in tufts all over his face. His hairdo was a bird's nest. "What are you doing?" he asked. "Why are you blocking the entrance to my home?"

"I'm waiting for someone."

"Who?"

"Just somebody."

This didn't seem to satisfy him. "On my doorstep?"

"On this corner, that's all."

He blinked at the rattler in its morbid wrapping, propped against the wall. "Is that what I think it is?"

"Probably."

"I haven't seen her in a while." He seemed genuinely disappointed.

"Me either," I said.

Dave Mizra locked and bolted his door with several keys. "When you see her, tell her I miss her music."

"Me too," I whispered, once he was already halfway up the block. I kept waiting. *One fifteen. One thirty. Two o'clock.* But Andrew Myers never showed up.

68. All Kinds of People

I lost count of how many times I dialled his number before he finally answered.

"Yeah, Myers. What's up?"

"Mr. Myers! Oh, great! It's Kaz Barrett, I'm sorry for calling so much but ..." (Why the hell was I *apologizing*?) "But you were supposed to meet me at noon today. Remember?"

"Are you the screenwriter who keeps calling? I thought I told you I wasn't—"

"No, we met this week when you brought some suits in. For dry cleaning. It's a place called the Sit'N'Spin. You came in and saw the—"

"Oh, shit, yeah! Sorry, kid, was that today we were meeting?"

"At twelve o'clock."

"Listen ..." His voice fell as he said the word. It dropped down to that minor chord you use when you're ashamed of something. Or when you're changing your mind.

"What is it?"

"Might be best if you and your friend just sit on that thing for now, okay?"

My chest tightened. I felt my most important parts grinding together, the gears stripping. "You said you wanted to buy it. You still do. *Right?*"

"I did some checking around, and I got it on very good authority that there's some people who might be trying to track the thing down."

"What people? The police?"

"I'm not sure, but no, probably not the police. It sounds like they know it's in town somewhere."

"So who? Like Shain Cope's family? Or someone else? *Who?!*" My voice was cracking into falsetto.

"Is it really true your friend was playing that thing in public? *On the street?* What is she, an idiot? Doesn't she know what it is?"

"No. I don't know. Maybe she doesn't—I mean, *didn't*. I don't know if I'm gonna see her."

Myers sighed. "Okay, kid, *listen*. I don't want to scare you or anything, but I'll tell you what I found out. Cope ran around with some pretty crazy guys out in LA. Bikers, dealers—*all kinds* of people. What I hear is that the Cope family have enlisted the help of some very heavy hitters." He paused. "If you ask me, this shit's going fubar, so do yourself a favour and tell your friend to *sit on it*. Don't take it out on the street. Don't show it to anybody. Just sit on it, okay?"

"*Wait,*" I said. Somewhere, I found a sliver of my regular voice. "I *need* that money, I really do. You told me—"

"We all need money, kid. It's what makes the world go round. But don't worry, I'll look you up when I'm in town again."

"*Again?* You're leaving?"

"I told you, I was only here a couple days. I'm sure we'll get to do business when things cool down."

"You can't. You promised!"

"I only said I was interested."

"But—"

"Look, I'm already on my way to the airport."

"No, wait! You don't understand, I wrote her a whole bunch of cheques! I really need that—"

Money, I thought.

I didn't say it out loud because there wasn't any point. Andrew Myers had hung up.

69. Seven Unanswered Texts and One Long-Ass Phone Message

2:04 p.m.

Zoey, BIG mistake! Don't cash the cheques. OK?

2:07 p.m.

Did you get my message?

2:08 p.m.

I can't buy this thing. I need the $ back. k

2:13 p.m.

EMERGENCY. Please call me!

2:32 p.m.

Seriously. We could both b in DEEP shit. Both of us! Just call me.

2:49 p.m.

Zoey, wtf? ANSWER YOUR PHONE!

3:00 p.m.

OK ... the truth: I lied. I screwed up. I made a mistake. Just call me. I need to tell you something.

3:05 p.m.

I dialled Zoey's number. "Zoey, it's Kaz. I really need to talk to you. I know I said I was an honest person, but the truth is I'm not. I mean, I am, but I wasn't—not when it really mattered. So I'm gonna tell you everything, okay? I'm gonna be honest, just like you said. But first, I have to say that I know you weren't completely honest with me. I know you didn't build that instrument yourself. I don't know how you ended up with it, and I don't care. Maybe you found it, maybe someone gave it to you, but maybe what you don't know is that it once belonged to Shain Cope ... yes, *that* Shain Cope. *He made it.* I know it sounds crazy, but it's true. When you left it with me that time, this guy came into my work, this movie producer from LA, and he knew it as soon as he saw it. He offered me *a ton of cash* to buy it and I should have split it with you, but I guess I was mad because you never told me the truth. So I bought it off you instead and I'm *so sorry.* But now I'm in huge trouble. Maybe we both are. It turns out Shain Cope's family sent some very bad people—like bikers or something—to get his instrument back. They may've been watching us, so please, *please* be careful. The guy said it was too dangerous for him to buy it right now. So, um, that's another reason I'm calling. Because I need the money back. Because there's something else I didn't tell you. That money I was saving wasn't for school. My marks are shit. I'll never get in anywhere. The real truth is, that money was for my mom. Remember how she acted when you met her? It's cuz she has this disease. It's called *somnitis* and it's super rare and it basically means she has these comas. They just happen, and someday, she's just not gonna wake up. I was saving that money to get her into a special clinic in New York. So you see? I need it back. The money I gave you. I *really* need it back. So please call me, okay?"

70. Memento Mori

I took an eastbound streetcar all the way across town. In the brightness of the afternoon, the unfinished apartments looked worse than I remembered.

I buzzed Zoey's apartment a million times (give or take). Eventually, an old man came hobbling out of the building. When he opened the door, I slipped inside. I bashed on Zoey's door, yelling for her to open up. It wasn't long before that same old man came back—this time with a security guy. I told them Zoey was my girlfriend, but neither of them cared. The guard told me to get lost.

I sat on the gravel out front and waited. But then something occurred to me. Why hadn't I thought of it before? There was another way to find her. So I hopped on the first streetcar going back the other way.

Falconer College gets made fun of a lot in the *Chronicler*. The most common slur is to call it one endless parking lot and, walking across the grounds, I had to agree the criticism was apt. Everything there was the same shade of grey.

When I asked the man at the reception desk, he said he had never heard of the Philosophy of Music Department.

"We don't have one of those."

"What about just a philosophy department?"

"Are you a student?"

"I'm looking for someone. I need to find Professor Zamani. He should be—"

"We don't have 'professors' at Falconer. We have instructors."

"Okay, *Instructor* Zamani."

The guy typed the name and then shrugged. "Sorry, I don't have that name in the system."

"Can you check by course? He teaches a course called Philosophy of Music."

The guy squinted at his screen. "Oh, wait, sounds like one of the weird adult ed courses, which means he'll be a sessional. So if he's anywhere, he's in here." He took out a big blue binder and flipped through an index of names in the opening section. "Here we go. *Paul Zamani*." He tapped the page, shaking his head in wonder. "No kidding. He teaches Philosophy of Music and—" He snorted. "*Jazz Appreciation*. I can't believe we do a course called Jazz Appreciation."

"Is he here? Where can I find him?"

"You might be in luck. It says he keeps office hours this evening."

I followed the directions to another building. Paul Zamani's room didn't have a name on it, just the number. When I knocked, a voice said, "Yeah-yeah, come in."

Zoey's father sat facing the door, reading a science fiction novel. His feet—in a pair of scuffed brogues, the left one half devoid of its sole—were propped up on his desk, which had nothing on it but a red pen.

He was thin like Zoey, with her same sharp features. His dirty-blond hair was swept back from his head, making him resemble a bird of prey, an eagle or a falcon. A tattoo of a robot wrestling a gorilla tumbled out from under his rolled-up sleeves. Both his ears were punched full of metal, the most prominent bauble being that of a grinning silver skull.

Everything about Paul Zamani fit with my idea of Zoey, but not in the way I expected. He looked so *young*, more like someone Zoey would hang out with, not someone who would help her with her homework.

"Mr. Zamani?"

"Yeah? Can I help you with something?"

I didn't quite know how to start. For a moment, I stared dumbly, mesmerized by the shining skull that dangled at his jawbone.

"Memento mori," he said.

"What?"

He put the book down and brought one hand to his ear. "It reminds me to live a full life because no matter what we do, one day we'll all end up like this." He cocked his head sideways, flicking the skull with a fingertip. "You in one of my classes?"

I shook my head. "I'm in high school. But I know your daughter. We've been hanging out. I bought something off her. Her instrument, actually, which I'm sure you know about, but it turns out I can't—"

"Waaay-way-way-way-wait. What did you say? My *daughter?"*

"Zoey."

He yanked his feet off the desk and leaned forward, smiling like this was all a joke. "I don't even *know* anybody called Zoey."

"Yeah, you do … she's …"

Your daughter?

The words wouldn't come out. They were stuck in all the gaps in my head, gaps that were just becoming clear as

I stood there, gaps like the missing pieces in an unfinished puzzle.

Paul Zamani shook his head. "You have *so* got the wrong guy."

"But … wait …"

"Do I *look* like somebody with a kid?"

"She told me she was your daughter."

"*Who* did?" He was more serious now.

"Her name is Zoey."

"And how do you know this girl? She go to your school?"

I shook my head. "You can't miss her, she's … she's …" I didn't know how else to put it. "*She's beautiful*. Kinda goth, kinda punk, and bright blue eyes. And dreads, all dyed pink and pur—"

"Oh, wait. Zoey Jones!"

"*Jones?*"

"That was *months* ago. She enrolled in my class last term, but she never paid her fees so after a couple weeks they booted her out." He looked down and nodded to himself. "But you're right. I know I'm not supposed to say this sort of thing, but yeah, I agree. She was quite … striking."

I nodded.

"She said I was *her father?*"

I nodded again.

"Why'd she tell you that? It's impossible. How old is she? Like, *twenty?*"

"Twenty? Really?" Could she be that old?

"Anyway, I am *definitely* not her dad."

When he said the word *dad*, something tightened in my chest. It was the biggest hole in the puzzle, and I had found the piece that fit.

"No," I said. "You're not."

"Well, that was easy. What convinced you?"

"You can't be Zoey's father. Because I've already met him."

71. The Truth about Zoey Zamani

She wasn't real.

72. The Girl Who Didn't Exist

"Who's the victim?" asked the woman behind the desk at the police station.

"Me."

"How old are you, son?"

"Almost seventeen."

She asked if I wanted a parent or guardian to be there while I gave a statement and I told her *no way*. She took me into a small, yellow room with a computer hooked up to a camera that recorded everything. Before I got very far with my story, however, she stopped me.

"There's another officer who'll want to talk to you," she said. "Someone from the fraud squad. Detective Singh."

She left me alone for a while, and when the door opened again, this huge cop came in. "I hate to break this to you," he told me, after I had explained much of my story, "but it's unlikely we'll get your money back. At least not for some time."

"Okay," I said, speaking slowly, trying not to hyperventilate. On the way to the police station, I had already braced myself for the possibility that Zoey would be untraceable, that I might never see my savings ever again. If that happened, I had a plan.

"Let's say it's really gone and we really can't get it back. Do you know if there's a reward for returning Shain Cope's instrument? Like maybe from his family?"

Singh shook his head. "We can check, but I don't think it'll do much good. I'm fairly certain that instrument you have is a fake."

"*A fake?*"

"This girl you met, Zoey, she said she made it herself. I imagine she did. It's probably the one true thing she told you." He turned the computer screen to face me and clicked around until he brought up a bunch of scanned documents. "The Shain Cope robbery was cleared up years ago. Everything was recovered, including two missing instruments, but the family didn't want to publicize the recovery because they thought it might encourage copycat thieves."

Singh showed me photographs of the recovered instruments. A saxophone made from plumbing pipes, and a second one— *shaped like a cross*. Stranger still, *it was tiny*. Compared to the object I knew as the "rood rattler," the thing in the picture looked like a child's toy. It was little more than a maraca in the vague shape of a crucifix.

Next, I scrolled through mug shots on the computer. We started with the women, but I didn't find Zoey. The men were next. It took almost an hour, but I finally found him. Zoey's father.

His face was clean shaven and his hair was shorter and bleached white, but even without the sculpted goatee, I recognized him. It was Andrew Myers. Only that wasn't his real name. Just like Zoey Zamani, there was no such person. His real name was Philip Konig. His file showed that he had a daughter named Zoey.

Zoey Konig.

"The fiddle con," Detective Singh whispered.

"What?"

"It's an old con game. People pulled it seventy or eighty *years ago*. The trick was to convince somebody to buy a famous violin, which of course was a cheap fake. But if you can play it—I mean *really* play it, really make it sing—then even a cheap fake can sound like a Stradivarius." He puffed out his cheeks and exhaled. Stale, warm breath hit me in the face. "*Amazing.* I didn't think anybody pulled stuff like this anymore." The look of utter stupefaction on his face told me what he really meant: *I didn't think anybody was dumb enough to fall for something like this anymore.*

Singh explained that Philip Konig was a thief and a con artist. He spent his life criss-crossing the continent—and much of the world—staying afloat pulling scam after scam. He had been arrested several times, along with his girlfriend, a woman named Evelyn. *Zoey's mother.* The files contained reports from social workers, too. These were from eight or nine years ago, when Evelyn consulted with them while Philip was serving time.

Evelyn told the social workers she no longer wanted to live life on the run, but that Philip would never stop, that he was addicted to the thrill he got out of swindling people. Evelyn claimed she couldn't afford to raise a child on her own, so she left Zoey in a foster home and promptly vanished. Later, when Philip got out, he was able to convince a court to release Zoey into his care.

"The daughter takes over where the mother left off." Detective Singh closed his eyes, massaging the bridge of his nose. "He probably taught her everything he knew."

Seeing the list of aliases made me think of something.

"*Wait*, I wrote that cheque to Zoey *Zamani*. It's not her name. She shouldn't've been able to cash it, right?"

Singh took a deep breath. "They would have had a dummy account, opened it with forged ID. Elementary stuff for someone with Konig's record." Detective Singh clasped his large hands and set them gently on the desk. "What I don't get is, *why you*? You're just a kid. Konig goes after wealthy immigrants and retirees. Easy targets, people with money who don't understand the system."

"I don't understand *anything*."

"I hope you do now."

"Maybe, but—*wait*. Immigrants!"

"So?"

"Dave Mizra."

The detective was baffled. "I'm sorry, *who*?"

"A guy who sells jewellery across the street from where I work—where I *used* to work. His name's Dave Mizra, and we used to think he was the richest guy on our block." Another piece of the puzzle was falling into place. "Oh, shit. *He's* the one they were after. They probably thought he was rich. They would've seen the Shain Cope posters in his shop. This was all about hooking *him*, not me. At least not at first."

I remembered the night I stared in at the shadowy poster of Shain Cope. Zoey had snuck up on me. *Planning a robbery?* she asked.

She really had been.

Then there was what "Andrew Myers" had said on the phone. *If you ask me, this shit's going fubar.* Fubar. I never made the connection, but now I saw he was right. Right then, it was a good way to describe my life: Fucked Up Beyond All Recognition.

In the computer files Singh showed me, there was one picture of Zoey. It had been taken when she was twelve or thirteen, just after she was placed in foster care. In the photograph, she was standing in the midst of a frumpy family in some anonymous suburb. There was a mom, a dad, a kid brother. Zoey's hair was different. It was a deep, chocolatey brown, full of waves and ringlets. The wind had caught one wisp and blown it across her forehead, just like one of her dreads. While everyone else was looking at the camera, Zoey's eyes squinted up at the sky. Her thoughts floated with the clouds, and I couldn't help wondering, was it the same with me?

Every moment we had spent together, had her mind been somewhere else?

73. *Clair de Lune*, Part 2

On my way home from the police station, I couldn't get Zoey out of my head. The brightness of her eyes. The slight downward turn of her mouth. Her hair. Her throat. The tattoo at the small of her back. I'd never be able to forget any of it, no matter how much it hurt me to remember.

When I was almost home, I saw A-Man was coming out of the Sit'N'Spin, a bag of towels bulging under both arms.

"Told you he'd be back. B-Man, I mean." He scowled into the street. "Some asshole hit Razor with his car."

"I know," I said. "I met him in the park."

A-Man nodded. "Dog's dead. B's pretty down about it."

"I'm pretty down myself."

"Yeah, we heard you got fired." He glanced back inside. "Would'ja believe John offered me the job?"

"He did?"

"I didn't take it. Wouldn't be right. Anyway, poor guy can't live without you. Give him a couple weeks, he'll hire you back."

"You think?"

"Sure. Sit tight, you'll see."

As I started up the stairs to our apartment, a strange thing happened. I heard music—and not just any music. I heard the slow unmistakable keen of the rattler, its bow sawing across the strings.

"*Zoey?*"

I really said her name out loud. The song was *Clair de Lune*—so it had to be her. But when I burst in, it wasn't Zoey playing the rattler. It was my mother.

"*Oh, Kaz! I love it!*"

Mom was sitting on the couch, the instrument propped between her knees like a cello. "I can't believe your friend could bear to part with it. *It's amazing.*"

Nomi knelt on the carpet at Mom's feet. "I'm sorry," she said. "I know you wanted to wait to give it to her, but I thought it would make her happy, so ..."

It had worked. Mom hadn't played a single note in years, yet here she was, doing just that. There was colour in her face, and she looked strong and focused in a way I could hardly remember.

"Come," she said, putting out one arm.

I sat beside her and she clutched me in a one-handed hug. My arms were around her waist, limp like a baby. I could smell the musty wood and metal of the rattler on her other shoulder.

"Thank you," she whispered. "This is the nicest thing you could have done for me. I'd forgotten what it felt like to make music." Her voice had started to crack. "The nicest, nicest thing."

When she said that, I don't know why, but I cracked up, too. Two tears leaked out, taking me completely by surprise.

"Kaz, what is it? What's the matter?"

I just shook my head and let her hug me again. How could I explain how badly I screwed up? How could I tell her that my savings were gone? How could I tell her that the strange instrument she had just been playing, the very thing that made her so happy, was at the centre of it all?

"It's about your job, isn't it? John fired you."

I sat up straight, sniffling. Nomi was staring at us from the floor, wide-eyed. "You know about that?"

Mom nodded. "I spoke to Mr. Rodolfo today. Doesn't seem like he's willing to re-hire you, but don't worry—smart kid like you, you'll find something else."

"Maybe."

Mom stared at me. "It's not just about that, is it? It's that girl, too."

I didn't answer.

"If she's too dumb to see how wonderful you are, then she doesn't deserve you."

Maybe I was crying because I was happy. Maybe it was because Mom looked better than I had seen her in a long, long time. Maybe all she needed was to play music again. Maybe, in a way, that was the cure.

"You look a lot better," I said.

"I am. Thanks to you."

I stood up. "That's good, but I'm pretty tired. I'll be in my room."

I don't remember falling asleep. When I did, it was black and bottomless. I slept all the way through dinner and didn't wake up until the next morning.

Mom was sitting on the bed beside me. She looked even better than the day before, smiling down, stroking my hair like I was a baby.

"Wake up, sleepyhead. We're going to Beauhaven."

74. The Last Time I Saw Her, Part 2

We drove up in silence. Nomi picked up on my grim mood (not a difficult thing) and kept quiet in the back seat. The air outside was humid and heavy. It was one of those dark days that come at the end of summer, when the sky goes all ashy and you just want it to rain and get it over with, but then it never does. Above us, there were layers of cloud so dark they looked like streams of soot.

All I could think about was Zoey. I thought about how strange she had acted the second time she wanted to stash the rattler at the Sit'N'Spin. All that looking over her shoulder, telling me the police were after her for busking on the street. It had all been a lie. I thought about all those questions about honesty.

I can trust you, right?

You're an honest person, yeah?

You've always been honest with me?

Then there was the way she had grabbed my wrist, just before I signed everything away to a girl who didn't exist. She had said it one last time.

Seriously. Be honest. You're really sure?

I had been.

But now I knew what it was all about. It was a test. In her own way, she was warning me. An *honest* person would never have signed that cheque. An *honest* person would have walked away as soon as he found out the thing he was buying was stolen—from some famous singer who had killed himself. An *honest* person would have called the police. Just like she had said at the movies that night, *You can't con an honest man.*

I steered us into the Beauhaven parking lot. Everything was calm and still. A huddle of parked cars reminded me of pigs, feeding from a trough around the building. The wide-openness of everything—the huge expanse of asphalt, the lack of tall buildings—made it seem like there was nothing to hold up the sky. I felt an endless sheet of dull grey plastic, settling over everything. I could hardly breathe.

"You look pale," Mom said, once we had joined the wallow of cars. "You should come in."

I shook my head.

"Give it another chance. Tracey really is—"

"*A genius.* I know, but I don't feel like it. Leave me alone, okay? Let me stay in the car."

Mom sighed and gave up. She and Nomi went in without me. I shut my eyes, resting my head on the steering wheel. Had I ever screwed up this badly before? This went way beyond letting your marks slip, or passing out at a party, or falling for the wrong girl. This was *serious.* This was a deep, dire, game-changing sort of fuck-up. The only thing I wanted to do was keep it a secret. Which of course was impossible. Eventually, I'd have to tell Mom what happened.

The smell of cigarette smoke cut through my self-pity. I lifted my head and saw a woman smoking in front of Beauhaven.

She seemed to be staring at me, but when I met her gaze, she looked away. After one final puff, she tossed the butt of her cigarette in the bushes and climbed into a minivan two spaces over. As the vehicle pulled away, the OPEN sign at the ice cream shop next door reflected in the tinted windscreen. The word flashed on and off, sliding over the black glass. OPEN … OPEN … OPEN …

It wasn't until the woman had backed out of the spot completely that I saw what was parked behind it.

A red convertible. Empty.

I got out and went over, one eye on Beauhaven. Could it really be the same car? There were speckles of rust on the side. Hadn't Andrew Myers-Slash-Philip Konig's car been spotless? Hadn't it always sparkled in the sun? Or was that merely how I remembered it because I believed his lies? Maybe I never noticed the rust because he had always parked across the street?

There were cardboard boxes in the back seat, the tops folded shut. I opened the door and tugged one of them open. It was nothing I recognized, nothing that looked like black crinoline or pink leopard print.

I went around to the front. There was a dent in the car's bumper, scratches too. I crouched down and ran my fingers over the metal. I tried to picture the shape of Razor's body. The height of her head. The broadness of her back. Could this have been where she was hit?

Behind me, someone came out of the ice cream shop. It was a hippie girl with a shaved head and a flowery dress, carrying a pair of vanilla cones. She wore enormous sunglasses, even though the sky was the colour of old steel. When she saw me, one of the cones slipped, shattering on the pavement.

"Zoey," I said. "Zoey … *Konig.*"

She didn't answer.

You could measure a girl's beauty by how she looked without any hair. That was what she told me. Now I knew she was right. Even shorn of every dreadlock, she still looked as sharp and beautiful as ever. Maybe even more so.

"How did you know we'd be here?" she asked.

"Are you gonna give me my money back?"

She took off the sunglasses. "I got your messages, but my dad burned the phone. I'm so sorry. Why didn't you tell me about your—"

"I'm calling the police." I took out my phone, called up the number and showed her the screen. "Give me back the money or I press Send."

"Wait, don't."

"You completely screwed me over and … and …" I was surprised by watery snot suddenly flowing down the back of my throat. "*Fuck!* I really liked you."

"Look at me. I'm a freak."

"Just give me back the money."

"I can't."

"Yes, you can. You have it and you can give it back."

"I *don't* have it, my dad does. I never have anything."

"So get it from him."

"I will, just not now."

"*It's for my mother!*"

Zoey threw down the other ice cream cone. "Why didn't you tell me? If I'd known, I would've … I mean, don't you tell people *anything*?"

"I do, but—"

"If you had told me, I never would've let my dad know about your savings. Even if he found out, even if he'd wanted to, I would've stopped him. You should've told me." She ground her teeth and looked down at the blob of vanilla melting at her feet. "Now it's too late."

I looked behind me at Beauhaven. "Is he in there now? Getting his *massage* or whatever?"

She nodded.

"That gun I saw, is it in the car?"

Her expression changed. "What? Why?"

"Give it to me."

"I'll get your money back. I promise. Just not right now. You have to believe me."

"How can I?" I went to the side of the car and opened the box again. "Where is it?"

"What're you gonna do?"

"Maybe I'm gonna kill him. If he doesn't give back what's mine."

"He'll kill you first. He's stronger than he looks. He'll do it with his hands."

"Is that where you got those bruises? Is that why you help him?"

"I promise I'll get you everything back, you just have to tru—*oh, shit!*"

I turned around and saw him coming down the steps from Beauhaven. He was in jeans and an old hoodie. For a second, I thought he had shaved his head as well. But no, he had merely bleached his hair. It was like it was in the mug shots. This time he had done his beard, too, even his eyebrows. It made his skin look pale, almost see-through. Teeth and eyes leaping out of a flat, white skull.

"Da'fuck is this now?"

His voice, gruff and threatening, was as altered as his face.

He pounded down the steps, but stopped dead when he saw who I was. His eyes flashed at Zoey.

"I didn't tell him, I swear!" she said. "It's his mom, she comes here, too. I told you! *She's sick.*"

He almost laughed. "Not if she comes here, she isn't. Not really."

"What did you say?" I was ready to do what Zoey said he'd do to me. Kill him with my hands.

"Don't sweat it, kid," he said. "It's just business. Wasn't like it was that much. What was it? Ten grand?"

"It was everything I had."

He shrugged. "Your loss." He made a move toward the car, but I cut him off.

"Fuck you! I'm calling the police."

I brandished the phone like a weapon and pressed Send.

Zoey's dad lifted the bottom of his hoodie and pulled out a *real* weapon. The gun I'd just asked for.

"Gimme your phone," he said. "Right now."

I didn't. In my ear, a recorded voice asked what I needed: *"Fire, police or ambulance?"*

"Police," I said.

Zoey's dad stepped forward. "I'm going to *fucking shoot you!*"

A human voice: *"Yes, what is your emergency?"*

"I'm at the Beauha—"

In one swift motion, Philip Konig stepped forward, grabbed my wrist, twisted it so hard my knees gave out and I doubled over. I dropped the phone and watched helplessly as his heel shattered it to bits.

"Next time," he growled at Zoey, "when I tell you to stay in the car, do it."

Zoey didn't move.

Her dad pointed the gun at her. *"Get in the car!"*

When he shouted, his grip on my wrist tightened. I yelped and, almost by instinct, took a swing at him with my free hand. With his attention on Zoey, I caught him by surprise. I connected just below his eye. It felt like I'd broken every bone up to my elbow.

The next thing I knew, Zoey's dad had one hand around my throat.

"You stupid little puke. We never *stole* your money. You wrote us a fucking cheque! You weren't robbed, you were *conned*. If you were a little swifter, you'd see the difference!"

I tried to say something, but I had no air.

"Dad, stop!"

Everything was turning grey. The sky roared in my ears. I heard a grunt. A scream. My body shook and jostled and fell. I landed hard on my hands and knees, and when I looked up, Zoey was down exactly like me, like an animal, like a spooked cat. The arch of her back juddered up and down. She was crying.

I tried reaching for her, but her dad picked her up around the waist and jammed her, kicking and screaming, into the car.

"I'll send it all back!" she shouted. "I promise!"

Oddly, the only thing in my head was *I never took a picture with her*. I'll never see her again. It didn't help that she had her face buried in her hands.

"Don't look, Kaz," she said, or at least that's what it sounded like. Her words slurred through her fingers. But how could I *not* look at her?

I breathed deeply and colour returned to the world. I saw Zoey, her face still hidden, as her dad shifted into reverse.

"Wait!" I said stupidly. "Let me see your face!"

She took her hands away.

"I'm sorry," she gargled at me. "I'm sorry!"

Her nose was smashed and her upper lip was split so wide it looked like she had two of them. Her dad must have hit her bad, probably with the butt of the gun. There was so much blood she looked like something in a horror movie—*and I was just staring at her*. I wasn't passing out.

I was cured!

I was so shocked by my lack of fainting, I didn't say or do anything. I just knelt on the blacktop like an idiot, watching dumbly as Zoey's mangled face sped away forever.

Then I discovered my miracle cure was only temporary. Lying a short distance off was one of Zoey's teeth. It stood out amid the wreckage of my phone, still clinging to a pink shred of her gums. A creeping whorl of melted ice cream came to mingle with the red.

Seeing that bloody scrap of her mouth brought on a familiar feeling. The roaring in my ears returned and the world went as black as the rivers of soot raging across the sky.

75. Cinnamon and Mould

When the world came back into focus, I was laid out on a slab of vinyl. The lights were dim, every wall was the colour of mouldy bread, and all I could smell was cinnamon. Tracey's face grinned down at me like a billboard.

"Relax," she cooed. "You're going to be fine."

That was hard for me to believe since her only treatment involved waving the same old metallic cylinder over my face. The smoke puffing out of it *reeked* of cinnamon.

"Are you okay?" Mom was standing on the opposite side of the massage table. "What happened just now?"

"I screwed up," I told her.

"Poor Nomi. I think she's traumatized. She found you lying in a pool of blood! And she found this." Mom held up Zoey's tooth. It looked like a chip of bone, like something that had fallen off the rattler. When I saw it, I felt a bit woozy.

I shut my eyes. "The tooth's not mine. I just fainted when I saw it."

"Thank god. As if we can afford emergency dental surgery. You want me to throw it out?"

"No, I wanna keep it."

Mom squinted at me. "Since when do you collect people's teeth?"

"I just want it, that's all." I reached over and clumsily grabbed it from her.

"I think you'd better tell me what happened."

So I did. I told Mom everything.

The first thing she did was call the police. Two officers from the West Olsten PD showed up with a lot of questions. They only took me seriously after I told them to call Detective Singh. They said it wouldn't be long before they found the dented red convertible. I hoped they were right, but this time, I had a feeling Zoey was gone for good.

While they asked their questions, the sky grew darker and darker. By the time the cops let us head home, it was pouring with rain. Off in the distance, there were flashes of lightning. Mom and I drove in silence nearly the whole way, fat drops of rain splattering the windscreen. The whole time I kept passing the tooth back and forth from hand to hand. I couldn't stop touching it.

Eventually, Mom said, "You saved all that money, just for me?"

I told her how badly I had let my marks slip. How I had basically given up on a lot of things since her attacks started.

"I don't want anything to happen to you."

"I know," she said, "but one day it will, no matter what we do. That's why it's so important you and Nomi get a good start in life. It's more important than anything that happens to me."

"That's not true."

"Have you ever thought that maybe I don't want to be cured?"

"Of course you do," Nomi said from the back. "You'll get better."

I nodded. "Nomi's right. You shouldn't say stuff like that."

Mom didn't say anything for a while. "You two have to understand something. Sometimes life gives you something and, even though it's not the most pleasant thing in the world, it's yours. Of course I want the attacks to stop, but if they don't, I'll deal with it. We'll all deal with it. And there's something else you need to understand. When I'm asleep for so long, I sometimes have dreams. Dreams like nothing else. They're so vivid, *so real*. They're the only place I still see your father."

What could I say to that? I remembered Mom's face when we rode with her in the back of the ambulance, on that day I first saw Zoey. All that orange padding, all mashed around her head like a vise, pressing her cheeks into doughy lumps. In spite of it all, I remember how nothing could stop her from smiling.

"But no," she said, "you're right. Let's see if we can plan a trip to New York. The least I can do is see what this doctor has to say. Even if we can't afford it, I owe you that much." She reached over and squeezed my hand in hers, pressing Zoey's tooth deep into my palm.

76. Echoes

Dave Mizra never came back for his CD. One morning, the windows at Fire & Ice were pasted over with newsprint. Dave Mizra was gone. I don't know if he went back to his wife, or if he opened another shop somewhere else. I never saw him again.

Then, in the middle of August, three cop cars pulled up just below our apartment. The lights flashed but there was no siren. My first thought was they had found them, Zoey and her father. I figured they had recovered my money. But when I went down to the street, I saw the Brothers were locked in the back of one of the cruisers. They looked pale and tired, but every bit as stone-faced as ever.

They brought Mr. Rodolfo out in handcuffs. He cursed and kicked and hollered at them, but the moment he saw me, it all stopped.

"What're you looking at?"

I shook my head. "What's going on?"

Mr. Rodolfo looked down at the pavement. "I was just trying to get by. What's so wrong with that?"

I figured Zoey had been right. Mr. Rodolfo really had

been running illegal gambling games, operating some sort of money-laundering scheme. But no, that was yet another thing I was wrong about.

It turned out the Brothers had been dumping dry-cleaning chemicals into the lake, rather than paying to dispose of them in the proper way. Some people living nearby had gotten sick, and there was a good chance all three of them would serve time in jail.

By the end of summer, it seemed like the only ones left were A-Man and B-Man. They still wandered the streets, rolling their die, muttering almost-comprehensible babble about machines and pinions, wheels and echoes.

B-Man found himself a new dog. It was a different breed of mutt, less threatening, with a smaller head and a slack mouth that always hung open in a goofy grin. Nevertheless, he gave it the same name. Razor. When I asked him why, he told me to look into the dog's eyes.

"See what I mean?"

I didn't.

"The eyes. They're the same."

"As ...?"

"Razor's!" He crouched down and yanked the dog's head to put himself face-to-face with the mutt. "Can't you see it? He's the old girl's ghost. He's her echo." He closed his eyes, rubbing the dog's skull. "You can hear it. Can't you?"

Maybe I could, but the echo I heard was a different one.

I ripped the Shain Cope CD onto our computer and put it on my phone, too. I listen to it sometimes, just staring at Zoey's tooth, which sits on the shelf above my desk, right where A-Man's die used to be. Every week, it turns a little more grey.

"Colt's-Tooth Blues" is still my favourite song. Every time I hear it, I notice things in the lyrics. My brain picks out little coincidences behind the words. I know it's impossible, but sometimes it seems like Shain Cope was trying to send me a message. A warning. Sometimes, I can't help thinking that he wrote his most famous song especially for me.

77. A Person of Interest

Just after school started again, a package came in the mail. It was a brown paper envelope, padded with stuffing and mummified in clear packing tape. There was no return address, but the sloppy collage of stamps were from England. When I tore it open, it was full of money. Soft, wrinkly British pounds. A lot of them.

"It's from her," Mom said when she saw it, and I knew she was right.

Inside was £810, a lot of money, but it fell far short of what I had lost. There was no note, nothing to identify the sender. The only other thing in the envelope was a clipping from another paper in the Chronicler chain. The *Over-the-Rhine Chronicler*. I thought Over-the-Rhine sounded like it might be somewhere in Europe, but when I looked it up, it turned out to be in Cincinnati. The headline was "Grifter Comes to a Violent End," and it said:

Philip Alan Konig, 48, a career criminal with a history of theft and fraud, was found dead last night in a rented apartment on West Liberty. Konig had been shot twice in the chest. The weapon, possibly belonging to Konig himself, was recovered at the scene. Police believe the fraudster may have been murdered by one of his former victims or by someone he was actively engaged in swindling. They are currently seeking the whereabouts of his daughter, Zoey Konig, 19, as a person of interest.

I don't know why, but something about the package made me want to start again, to do things in a completely new way. Not that I ever had a system of doing anything at all. I hadn't. *I didn't.* That was my whole problem. I could have sat around, watching the mail slot, hoping and praying for another bundle of money to come tumbling through, but somehow that seemed wrong. I had to *do something.*

So I got on the bus.

Mr. Dearborn lived in the suburbs. It took an hour to get out there. He answered the door in cargo shorts and a faded apron that said, "Sometimes I'm off in my own little world, but that's okay, they know me there." His beard was thicker than I remembered.

He was a short guy, a couple inches shorter than me, and his face was creased all over, but not from age, more from smiling so much. He was in pretty good shape, too, apart from a pot belly. He looked like a jolly, domesticated elf—but one who worked out.

"Nice apron," I said.

"*Kaz?* What are you doing here?"

He looked worried. I wondered if other students had visited, too, come to tell him how they had been traumatized by the alt-porn he had shown us in health class.

"I need your help," I told him.

Alana had told me Dearborn wasn't teaching at a school anymore. He was doing private tutoring instead, which was exactly what I needed.

"I'm not sure what I can do for you."

"I heard you were tutoring."

He laughed. "At an ESL school in a shopping mall. I'd say your command of the language is a bit more advanced."

"Oh, I heard that …" I didn't know what to say.

"Did you come all the way from—"

"Evandale. Yeah."

"My wife and I were just about to eat. Why don't you join us." He rubbed his paunch. "As you can see, I have this tendency of making too much."

Mr. Dearborn's house looked the way I thought Zoey's apartment should have looked. Every wall was lined with bookshelves. There were novels, dictionaries, photography books, books about art, books about architecture, old magazines, even comic books and manga. We followed the smell of bacon into the kitchen.

Mr. Dearborn's wife was taller than him, with insanely long limbs, at least in my opinion. Two black pugs were curled around the legs of her chair. They started yapping at me.

"Who's this?"

I thought Dearborn's wife might be wary of me, but if she was, she hid it well.

"This is Kaz," Dearborn told her. "A former student. He's gonna join us for brunch. Kaz, this is Mrs. Dearborn."

"Call me Valerie." She reached out from what seemed like miles away and shook my hand.

"That's Sal and Dean on the floor. Would'ja please shut up, guys?" He bent to pat them and the dogs licked his forearm like he sweat gravy.

As we ate, I explained why I was there. With my money trouble, my only chance was to bring up my marks and shoot for a scholarship. I couldn't do that alone. Of course, when I told Dearborn how far my marks had slipped, he wasn't optimistic.

"Sounds like an uphill battle," he said.

"My mom really wants me to get into a decent school, and I want to make her proud." It was true. I was being honest, for once.

"You think you can do all this in one year?" Mrs. Dearborn asked me.

Mr. Dearborn shook his head. "Val's right. One year's not a lot of time."

"I can do it."

"Maybe. But why me? Last I checked, I hadn't really made it as a teacher."

"Are you kidding? You're the best one I ever had. Trust me, I learned *loads* from you."

"I'll bet you have!"

Dearborn grinned wickedly, first at me, then at his wife. That set us off. All three of us lost it, cracking up around the tiny breakfast table. Even Sal and Dean joined in, hopping and yapping around my feet. We just couldn't stop.

78. "Colt's-Tooth Blues," by Shain Cope (1981)

He heard there's rain in Paris
Gotta wonder if she's there
She always looked her prettiest
With drizzle in her hair
The sky's got nothing in it
Just the flapping of the crows
The sun's as bright as butterflies
Or so the saying goes

You wish that she were still around
You wish that she were here
I thought I was a poet once
(I'm just a profiteer)
If only I were beautiful
Like something rotten on a beach
That stuff has got a kind of grace
No one ever sees

There's a woman out in front of here
Selling pictures of the saints
Here's a wandering of pilgrims
Come to maunder their complaints
They dream about the good old days
They want a little fun
No one told them youth
It's only wasted on the young

Bet you wonder where she got to
Bet you wish that she was here
I could've been a poet once
I'll prob'ly disappear
Wishing I was pretty
In a way nobody sees
The way the dirt's as pure as gold
To the toes of any tree

Now the chimney pots are crumbling
The walls are caving in
You can always count on me
To take it on the chin
It's darker now, it's going grey
Hey look, here come the crows
That moon's a wicked stick of bone
Or so the saying goes

I wonder what she's doing now
If only she were here
I thought I was a poet once
Full of bourbon, full of beer
If I could get the words to bloom
I bet you I could sing
Without the mud of autumn rain
There's never any spring

She waltzed around, she beat her drum
She had her own guitar
All the time I used to think
The girl could be a star
Then she up and went away
Felt like I was cursed
Get it wrong or get it right
There's gotta be a first

If only you could see her now
If only she were here
Songs like this are all we got
These little souvenirs
I hope you think it's pretty
Like something forgotten on a beach
That stuff has got a beauty to it
No one ever sees

Acknowledgments

This book would not be possible without the efforts of many wonderful people. My sincere thanks to my family and friends, for their endless refrains of support and encouragement; to Lynne Missen, whose friendship and guidance made this story hum; to Jackie Kaiser, without whom I would lose all rhythm; to Mitch Kowalski and the chorus of voices at the Toronto Writers' Centre, where I wrote the majority of the book.

I would also like to thank the Ontario Council for the Arts, for the generous grant that allowed me to complete the initial draft. Finally, as always, my thanks to Machiko (who knows exactly where the laundromat is).